MOTHER MAYHEM

an Eden Creek Cozy Mystery, Book 4

—

JL VANDERBEEK

The Crafty Branch LLC

CHAPTER ONE

"Ugh! That's an awful place to end things!"

We had just finished up our evening binge-watch of *NCIS* on a cliffhanger of a season's ending. Jerri was right. It was an awful place to be left hanging, especially considering our next chance to catch up with Gibbs and crew wouldn't be for quite some time.

Pre-Christmas events were stacking up. Between her work functions, my work functions, community functions she would be on-duty for, and the various things to do, see, and be aware of, it'd be almost the New Year before we both had nights off at the same time. So, while it sucked to be left with a cliffhanger, I supposed it made sense in a karmic way.

I was on a bit of a cliffhanger, myself. Though Jerri didn't know it.

At the Dawson's for Thanksgiving dinner, I'd met Foster, a friend of Jerri's from high school. Friend and ex-girlfriend, to be more specific. And Foster all-but came out and said that Jerri liked me as more than a friend.

And I didn't know what to think about it.

Call me chicken, but I hadn't talked to Jerri about it yet. I didn't know where to begin. I also hadn't decided how I felt about the whole thing. I thought, for sure, I needed to figure out that part before I broached the subject. If Foster was right, and Jerri wanted a more romantic relationship, I needed to know whether that was something I wanted. And if she didn't, if Foster had just been winding me up? Maybe she was the type to play head games with total strangers for kicks. At any rate, if she was wrong, then I needed to know if I was okay with that or if I'd be disappointed.

Wait. There was a part of me that might feel disappointed that Jerri wouldn't be interested in me in that way? Since when?

Probably since that time she sat next to me in the Wilmar's pool house and I got all those butterflies in my stomach, a little voice reminded me.

For the time being, I silenced that voice. I didn't have time to deal with the potential friend-on-what-level quandary. I had to get ready for not only my first Christmas in Eden Creek, but also the first Christmas I'd spend with my actual biological family.

I'd eventually forgiven my boss for the awkward surprise reunion he'd orchestrated. While he apologized for embarrassing me in front of the entire department, I don't think he was in the least bit sorry that I was now getting to know the mother that gave me up when I was days old and the rest of her immediate family. That family included her mother and father, her husband, two children, and two grandchildren.

So far, I'd only been talking to Veronica, my mother. We'd emailed, texted, and even had a video chat once. That last one was so awkward we opted to stick to written communication for the foreseeable future.

At any rate, I'd agreed to spend some of my winter break with them, though I would be back on Christmas Eve to spend the actual holiday with Windi and Jasmine.

And Jerri. I mean, I was sure to see her at some point. She had a large family, and they all came home to spend Christmas with Mrs. Dawson, but I figured we'd meet up at some point between Christmas and New Year.

I mentally checked over the gifts I'd be bringing to said family. I'd sussed out enough information to avoid too much awkwardness, I hoped. Veronica's grandchildren were only three years old, so I'd gotten them activity books and a stuffed animal each. The men were getting bottles of liquor, the women bottles of wine. It was unoriginal, but classic, I hoped. They could always re-gift what they didn't like.

For the people I knew better, they were getting books. Yes, I was that friend. Books made awesome gifts, in my mind, and anyone shocked or dismayed by the prospect probably wouldn't be receiving one, anyway. I'd check on some of the special orders I'd placed through The Book Nook, our local used and new bookstore, in the morning.

"I'm off then," Jerri said, rising and stretching. "When do you leave for The Wilds?" She'd christened the Richardson/Moorehead home after one look at the picture Veronica had sent. It was only a couple hours away from here, but the giant, red log-cabin surrounded by trees and nothing else looked like it was nestled deep in the mountains somewhere farther north. "Will they have cell service? Broadband? Do we have time to get you a SAT-phone before you go?"

"Hilarious. Five days. And it only looks like no-man's-land. They're not all that far from Jackson, and there's stable cell and satellite signals at the house. I will not be in the boonies."

"If you say so."

I looked up at her. The apartment was too small to make walking a guest to the door a necessary or practical thing. Besides, Jerri had come-and-go privileges, so it wasn't like she didn't know the way. Even so, looking up at her from my seat on the sofa brought back those questions I was trying not to answer just yet. I felt self-conscious and looked away.

Then froze as Jerri bent down and hugged me.

"Just thought I'd give you your going-away hug now, in case I don't see you before you leave."

CHAPTER TWO

Eden Creek took pride in its displays of seasonal cheer. For Christmas, each light post and stop light were decked out in red and white tinsel garland, with lighted candle shapes at the tops. In the crepe myrtle trees that lined Main Street you could see small, soft-white lights wound through the branches and larger balls of lights that looked like illuminated ornaments when they turned on at dusk.

The Downtown Business Association sponsored a window decorating contest, encouraging residents and visitors alike to drop the names of their favorite storefronts in boxes mounted to the light posts. The shops took this seriously and put tremendous effort into their displays. I was fortunate that I did not have to choose between loyalty and talent, as Windi's store—Penfeathers Stationery & Gifts—was truly outstanding.

The Book Nook had done a fair job of their own, of course, and I complimented Nicole on her decorations as I entered the store. They'd stacked red, green, and white-jacketed books into a tall pyramid before wrapping the whole thing in twinkling fairy lights and garland. Several books were tied with enormous bows under the makeshift tree as well.

"Good morning, MC."

"Morning, Nicole. I just wanted to check if the books I ordered had come in, yet."

"Not yet, and I told you to call me Nicki. They will definitely be in before Christmas," she assured me. "You don't have to ship any back out, do you? Because I could take care of that for you, too."

"No, they're for local folks. No worries there."

"Okay, hon. I'll give you a text when they come in."

I walked past the still-closed Penfeathers to stop at the Sip & C'est Café for a peppermint mocha and an eggnog scone. Teddy, the tow-headed son of shop-owners Molly and Joe, was behind the counter when I entered. He looked rather dashing in his Santa hat and matching apron, though he was far from having the bushy white beard to complete the look.

"Morning, Miss MC."

"Hey Teddy, how's it going?"

"Can't complain," he said with a smug grin.

"Do I even want to ask?"

"I don't know what you're talking about." Teddy had gotten a dubious popularity boost after being the sheriff's lead suspect earlier this year. He had not been responsible for or in any way involved in the death of one of their patrons, but the girls around town gave Teddy more attention after his brush with the law, and he'd become a far more self-confident man out of the ordeal.

Not that he'd played the field much. Once Genevieve, the granddaughter of my landlord, looked his way, he was smitten. The young couple could often be seen around town, completely besotted with one another.

"Uh huh. Sure," I said, placing my order. "Are you looking forward to classes starting next month?"

"Couple more weeks of freedom." Teddy joked, but the ordeal with Mrs. Winslow had also given him a career path outside of his family's café business. He'd taken an interest in law enforcement after his brief stay on the wrong side of a cell and would start at the local community college with the spring semester, thanks to a scholarship from his former grade school teacher.

Accepting my coffee and pastry, I took a seat at the table by the bay window, watching the citizens of Eden Creek pass by on their pre-holiday errands.

—

Not wanting to disturb Windi before the shop was open, I waited until a few minutes after ten o'clock to leave my spot at the Sip & C'est and stroll back down to her door.

"Is this visit business or personal?" Windi asked.

Windi had been my best friend since we met in college, and the reason I'd come to Eden Creek this summer. She'd been kidnapped and needed rescuing. She and her daughter, Jasmine, were also the reason I stayed, taking a job at Tulane as a research assistant to be nearby after her marriage ended. We now lived a stone's throw from each other, something we hadn't been able to claim since leaving college a decade ago.

"Bit of both, I'm afraid. I need a secret Santa gift for one of the TAs and I left it until the last minute. What would you recommend?"

"What do they like?"

"I have no idea. I've never even met him. He works with one of the other professors." I could guess he liked history, since that was the department we were in, but other than that, I had no clue. "I just need something… all purpose and worth around twenty dollars." I shrugged and threw myself at her mercy.

She rolled her eyes at me. "So, what you need is the Swiss army knife of gifts."

"Do you carry those?" Penfeathers carried plenty of things from stationery to scrapbooking supplies to frou-frou frilly things I'd never had a use for. I was taking a chance, albeit a calculated one, that she'd have something for an unknown, just-out-of-undergrad young man.

"I'm sure we can find something."

The petite blonde left the counter and headed toward the pen display. "Normally I'd prefer to know more about the recipient before suggesting a gift, but even with all our laptops and smart phones, we still need a reliable pen on the regular." She turned to face me. "Pick one."

The display wasn't huge, but it still felt a bit overwhelming. At first glance, most of the pens looked identical, but then small things began to stand out, like a spot-the-difference puzzle. In the end, I resorted to the always reliable close your eyes and point method (it was that or eeny, meeny, miny, moe) and then picked the one next to the one I'd pointed at, just to be contrary.

"Are you quite finished?"

"Yes, this will do fine." It had a gunmetal finish with bright silver hardware, a decorative swoosh on the clip, and looked very nice and shiny against its flocked backing. I made sure not to touch the pen itself for fear of leaving smudges on it.

"Would you like me to wrap it for you?"

"Yes, please." I loved my friend. While I could do a decent job at wrapping gifts, especially those that came in nice, regular box shapes, Windi was amazing at making things look just that next level special. Before long, I had a wrapped present for my secret Santa recipient and I had officially completed my holiday shopping more than a week before Christmas.

"So, what's the personal part?"

"The what?"

"You said this visit was both. Business and personal. What's the latest? Have you talked to Jerri yet?"

"She was over last night for pizza and *NCIS*." I hedged.

"Yes, but did you *talk* to her?" Windi was the only person I'd confided in about Foster's revelation. She'd known about Jerri's dating history, thanks to Bryce's friendships with the Dawson family going back to the cradle. She'd been more surprised that I hadn't known Jerri was a lesbian than by the fact, or suspicion, that Jerri could be interested in me as a romantic partner and not just a friend.

"We talked about stuff."

"You didn't ask her, did you?" How someone six inches shorter than me could give me a disapproving glance, as if from above, stymied me, but Windi managed to do just that.

"No. I haven't figured out how I feel about it yet. I can't bring it up until I know, and I can't know until I think about it myself, and I can't do that until after Christmas."

"And how are you feeling about meeting your family next week?"

"Nervous," I admitted.

"It's going to be fine, you know." She patted my hand as it rested on the counter. "They're going to be nervous, too, so you're on the same page. And you can leave if you get uncomfortable. Either check into a hotel in Jackson or drive on back home."

I'd considered the idea of home over the last couple of months, which was something I hadn't dreamed of doing before. I'd been on the move every two years or more since graduating college. Going from one job to another. One town to another. But Eden Creek had grown on me. I'd become close to the people here. Made friends. Felt like I might stay longer than usual.

And do what, I didn't know. That was a problem for future-me to sort out. Before then, I had family to face. And before that, I had to wrap up the semester's work with my boss, Professor Dunkirk.

But first, there was the town Christmas festival to enjoy.

—

Small towns seem to have a knack for celebrations. You might think larger cities are where it's at for the parties, but nothing I've seen anywhere else can hold a candle to the downright wholesomeness of the Eden Creek Christmas parade.

Oh, sure, there were local politicians and office holders smiling for votes or favor, but can you really be mad at them for horning in on a good time when they've got their kids and grandkids riding with them in convertibles, truck beds, or tractors? I certainly couldn't.

The high school marching band played a lusty, if not completely in tune, version of "You're a Mean One, Mr. Grinch." A neighboring parish's band passed us paying *Sleigh Ride* as a drum cadence. And the tiniest twirlers I'd ever seen had sparklers attached to their batons as they pranced by. Peppermints, candy canes, and beads rained along the sidewalk.

Pageant princesses from five different towns waved to us from their padded perches of polyester satin and crepe paper. And our very own Cynthia Truesdale, Miss Christmas Tinsel 2017, closed the parade as her horse-drawn carriage showered shaved-ice snow in her wake.

"They could have filmed this for any number of schmaltzy, made-for-television movies without changing a single thing."

"You know we have a lot of practice throwing parties down here," Windi said as we replaced our chairs inside Penfeathers before following the end of the parade to collect Jasmine from her dance school float. "We hold a parade every time a pig's born."

A slight exaggeration, but Louisiana towns definitely lived by the motto of any reason to party is a good reason to party. Even death was celebrated here, thinking of the Second Line tradition to both mourn and celebrate loved ones. I'd already seen two in New Orleans since the semester started.

Jasmine was rushing so fast for home with one of her fellow dancers she almost passed us in her hurry.

"Where's the fire?"

"Ginger dropped her retainer case when we were throwing out candy during the parade. We're gonna go find it!" Jasmine called out over her shoulder.

Windi and I exchanged a glance before turning and following the girls back to where we'd started.

"Do you remember where you dropped it, Ginger?"

"No ma'am. Not exactly," she said. Despite her name, the girl's hair was black as night, pulled up in its ballerina bun. "But I realized it was gone by the time we passed the Sip & C'est."

We searched up and down the parade route but found no sign of the hot pink retainer case.

"I'm sorry, Ginger. Somebody must have picked it up, thinking it was a throw. I'm sure your dad won't be too mad about having to get a new case," Windi tried to console the girl.

"No." She still looked mournful. "But he's not gonna be happy that my retainer was inside of it."

CHAPTER THREE

I was still chuckling over Ginger's dilemma Monday morning as I crossed the Causeway bridge over Lake Pontchartrain. Not her potentially getting in trouble, of course. More the way she'd buried the lead.

I'd escaped the need for braces or retainers, but some of my foster siblings hadn't been as lucky and it was never a good thing when the retainer got thrown in the trash or left on the bus. Windi felt certain it would turn up and promised to email all the schools and activity groups she had contacts for to ask them to be on the lookout for the missing mouthpiece.

Locking the Jeep after making sure I had the bag with my Secret Santa gift and the chips and dip I'd signed up to bring to the party, I headed in for the next to the last workday of the year.

Personally, I thought it would have been better to have the department party on Tuesday, but the powers that be wouldn't do that anymore.

"Oh, we tried that a couple of years ago. Too many people snuck out for the holidays before we could even get to the party, and the dean was quite put out that only a handful heard his speech." Professor Dunkirk shrugged. "No more waiting until the last day."

It just felt wrong to have a celebratory lunch and then work for another day and a half. Very Ebenezer of them, with all of us Cratchit's roaming the halls. Not that I was truly complaining. After all, working alongside academia meant I got all the school holidays off and a good part of the summer, too. It was a definite perk of my accidental career path as a research assistant.

All the perks of grad school. None of the debt.

Turning on the light in the closet that passed for my office, I saw that my own Secret Santa had already delivered their gift. The box was on the larger size and I stilled my hand, considering the potential of an ugly sweater hiding inside. There was nary a note or card on the outside, so I settled into my chair to brave the unveiling, grateful to be alone in case my face gave away an unfortunate reaction.

Santa was smart, as they'd wrapped each half of the box independently. Once I'd untied the bow, there wasn't even tape holding the two halves together. I gingerly lifted the lid and saw a beautiful wooden picture frame nestled inside golden tissue paper. It was ornately carved and polished, stained an ebony black, and held… my DNA results from earlier this year.

Professor Dunkirk was hovering in my doorway as I looked up.

"I hope you've finally forgiven me," he said, grinning.

I couldn't even pretend to be mad. "You know I already did. Thank you for the frame. It's lovely."

"Just something I like to do to keep my hands busy on the weekends."

"You made it yourself?"

"Same as all the rest on my wall." The professor had crowded one wall with pictures of family in a variety of frames. I hadn't realized they were all handmade by him, but they all shared certain hallmarks that, now that he mentioned it, made perfect sense.

I was doubly glad I'd splurged on the next size up bottle of Irish whiskey for his gift.

"I know you're not usually the touchy feely type, but can an old man request a hug for Christmas?"

I laughed as I scooted around my desk. I was getting more used to people who hugged, living down here. And hugging the professor was like hugging a living teddy bear. It was no burden at all.

"I'll see if I can replace the data with an actual picture later this week," I said as I stepped back.

"That's what I was hoping for, young lady." He almost looked to be getting teary-eyed.

Sentimentality ran rampant during the holidays, true, but Professor Dunkirk was a big softie. One of his interns had sent him a video, last week, about a rescued dog who'd been adopted and given the medical attention it needed, and I'd found him in his office sobbing over his phone.

I busied myself with settling the lid back on the gift box and placing it on the narrow slip of a shelf to my right so he could compose himself and we could go over our usual Monday business. Our meeting was brief, if only because of the short week ahead. We'd more than accomplished his goal of completing the lineage tracking of the family he was using to narrate his book.

In January, we'd officially begin the next phase of the project, the one where I started assembling his story notes and ephemera into sections and chapters so he could provide the narrative pieces along the way. At this rate, I doubted he'd need much of my help beyond the coming summer, far short of the two years my contract was for, but certainly not unheard of.

I had only a moment to consider asking what he would work on next before my Secret Santa recipient stopped by to thank me for their pen. As I'd hoped, Windi's suggestion was right on the money.

"So, Mary Catherine, is it true you're going to spend a week with your family during break?" Sondra asked, balancing a plastic plate on her cup of mulled cider.

"I leave tomorrow, right after work."

Professor Dunkirk's pre-Thanksgiving surprise of reuniting me with my mother had drawn quite the crowd, and those who hadn't witnessed it firsthand heard about it through the campus grapevine. Or they could have seen it in the department memo that went out upon our return from Thanksgiving break, as it had been the headline, complete with photographic evidence. The blessing and curse of cameras on every cell phone.

While it was an awkward way to meet the mother I hadn't even wondered about since I hit double digits, it was ultimately a good thing. While intent cannot always make up for impact—embarrassment, awkwardness, and being thrust into a family I hadn't looked for—nor should it be a get out of responsibility free card, I chose to take it as the gift he intended and be open to meeting my birth family.

"Oh, to be a fly on that wall," Sondra smirked. "I mean, what are you even going to say to them? What are they going to say to you?"

"Veronica and I have been emailing for a couple of weeks. It's not like I'm going in there blind."

"Of course not. But still. Who else will you be meeting?"

"Veronica's husband, her mother and father, and her daughter, son, and the daughter's two daughters."

"Don't you mean your stepfather, grandparents, half siblings, and nieces?"

CHAPTER FOUR

Sondra was technically correct. I had considered my connection to each of the people I'd be introduced to, but hadn't quite warmed to the idea of these veritable strangers on such intimate terms.

Veronica and I had talked about it the first time she referred to Maxine as "your sister" and I flinched. I think we were both fortunate that Veronica had been a school guidance counselor in West Virginia before her husband, Bruce, had gotten a job as a plant manager just outside of Jackson, Mississippi. She was easier to talk to when I thought of her in that role, and my request to stick to names instead of familial titles was respected.

The GPS chirped in my ear to turn off the highway at the next light, bringing me within fifteen minutes of my destination. The two hours on the road had not been nearly enough time to calm my nerves. I could feel my palms sweating against the microsuede steering wheel cover.

I pulled into the first gas station I saw. Was I stalling? Perhaps. But I rationalized it away, knowing the gas gauge was just above the quarter mark and it was always better to fill up and not risk forgetting the next time I got into the Jeep.

Ask me how I knew.

"Are you from around here?" a man on the opposite side of the pump asked.

"Sorry, no. Just passing through." Rule one of traveling alone was never to tell strangers where you were from or where you were going.

"Oh, it's just you looked kind of familiar. I thought I knew you from somewhere."

"Nope. Sorry."

It wasn't vanity that made me think he looked almost disappointed. More so than if the attempt at conversation had been a mere pick up line or con opening. I pretended to watch the numbers rise on the pump display and studied him from the corner of my eye.

Medium height, dirty blond hair, black windbreaker over a green, button-down shirt. His car was blue, four-door, but any more than that was hidden by the pump or the massive trash barrel and posts set between us. Just an average dude getting gas and talking to strangers.

For being only a short drive from the state capitol, the house looked just as isolated in person as it had in the picture I'd shown Jerri. The red wood stood in stark contrast to the tall pine trees bordering the home on three sides, with crisp white trim at the windows and eaves. The main structure was two stories, with the lower level extended to one side. A breezeway separated the main house and the extension.

I'd parked, but not yet shut off the engine. The moment I did I'd be committing fully to unlocking a part of my life I'd shut away to protect myself.

The opening of the front door decided for me.

Several people, faces I recognized from Veronica's photos, now stood at the deck railing, lit by the porch lights studded between the large windows. Time to rip off the bandage, get out of the car, go face the music, and all those other euphemisms for getting started. If for no other reason than to quit feeling like a wild animal on exhibit at the orphan zoo.

Not that I was an orphan any longer. That was the point of this, right? And the fundamental changing of one of the few constants in my life until a few weeks ago. Whatever. I'd sort it out later, after the introductions.

"You made it!" Veronica said, coming toward me. "I told the rest to stay put and not rush you all at once," she said in a softer voice as she neared and enveloped me in a hug.

"Thanks."

"Do you need help carrying anything?" She held her arms out to take whatever.

"No. I've got it." A lifetime of being on my own meant I was an expert at packing and organizing items so I wouldn't have to ask for help. Even if I ended up looking like a pack mule in the process. I was independent. That didn't have to change just because I had relatives now.

"Everyone back inside. No need to crowd out here when it's much more comfortable in the living room." Veronica herded her pack into the house ahead of me, the others subdued, waiting for their cues.

I set my suitcase, backpack, and tote full of gifts on a padded bench just inside the door. Even fiddled with an imaginary issue in one of the bags to stall for one more moment. One more breath.

"Well, let's get the introductions out of the way, shall we?" Veronica nodded at me. "This is my husband, Bruce," he said a soft hello and offered his hand. "My mother and father, Rosemary and Henry Richardson, and my son, Roger."

I shook hands with each and nodded acknowledgements.

"Maxine and the girls will be back in just a bit. They needed to run to the store for a couple of items real quick. Otherwise, the house wouldn't be this quiet." The group chucked and visibly exhaled at Veronica's comment.

"Unfortunately, Maxine's husband, William, is still offshore at the moment, so you might not get to meet him this visit, unless he can get back on land before you head back home." William worked on oil rigs in the gulf and was gone for large chunks of time. It was one reason the family shared the large, multi-generational home. The other was they were all just that close that they didn't want to be apart. Except for Roger, who'd taken a job on the other side of Jackson after college and had his own apartment there. They still kept a room for him here, though, for whenever he came to visit.

Even with the grandparents' suite across the breezeway, I had wondered how so many people could fit in one house without tripping over one another. What looked like a simple cabin from the front, however, turned out to be deeper than the surrounding trees made it seem.

"It's like the T.A.R.D.I.S., all bigger on the inside and everything."

"Those big, old-growth trees make kind of an optical illusion so you can't see how big the house really is," Veronica explained. "It used to be a vacation rental before we bought it, so it was built for large groups from the beginning. Bruce and I have the upstairs, the kids on the ground floor, and then Mom and Dad across the way."

"I hope I'm not putting anyone out or anything."

"Nonsense. Even with all of us here, we keep a guest room for visiting family or friends. I even have a murphy bed in my sewing room for any overflow and the sofa in the upstairs sitting area folds out. You are nowhere close to putting anyone out of anywhere."

She stopped to face me as we reached the guest room door. "I'm just so happy you decided to come stay for a while. I…" She placed a hand on my arm. "I realize it's not easy for you and I promise, no one expects you to accept us right off the bat. Any time you need to step away and process or sort yourself out, don't even worry about it. You do what you need to. Okay?"

I nodded. Her words reassured me. In the same instance, they spiked my nerves up all over again. They reminded me of some of the younger, more hopeful, foster families I'd lived with over the years. To get a similar speech in an unfamiliar house brought me right back to being twelve years old. I shook off the memory and concentrated on setting my bags down on the bed, finding the nearest outlet for my phone and laptop chargers, and unpacking my suitcase into the dresser kept empty for guests.

Veronica had vanished for a moment, but I heard her soft steps returning before long. She was holding a quilt in her arms when I looked her way.

"I wanted to give you this before things got too hectic. I've made one for each of my children, their partners, their kids. It's to welcome you to the family, officially." She held out the blanket to me as she took two shy steps into the room.

The quilt was a series of boxes with concentric squares inside. In shades of black, white, gray, and navy. Some of the fabric had tiny stars or flowers on them, but one had a print with rows of books, shelf after shelf of spines. I accepted the gift, which was heavier than it looked, and ran my hands over the patterns stitched on top of the blocks.

"Thank you. It's beautiful."

"I'm so glad you like it." She beamed at me. I felt like I should say more, but I had no clue what.

"You take as much time as you need to settle in and then, when you're ready, come back into the main room and we'll have supper."

Just then, we could hear the front door opening, followed by the voices and rapid footfalls of small children in the large space. Veronica looked over her shoulder. "That must be Max and the girls. I'll go help with them. Just take your time."

When she'd gone, closing the door behind her, I realized I hadn't had time to text my friends that I'd arrived safely. I lingered over that task and gave a cursory glance at my email. I even checked my hair in the mirror in a rare moment of vanity. Still red, straight, and pulled back into its usual ponytail. Taking yet another deep breath, I squared my shoulders and placed a steady hand on the doorknob that led into the family fray.

CHAPTER FIVE

Veronica and Maxine set out an enormous spread for the evening meal. Talk flowed easily around the table between bites. I fielded the expected questions about where I'd grown up and what I'd done after college, and what I was doing now. I felt sure Veronica would have passed some of that along since we'd covered a lot of the same topics in our emails, but even if they were asking only to be polite, it was kind of them.

In return, I did my best to ask polite questions when I could get a word in edgewise. Most of my answers led others to share their own experiences without prompting, making it more of a conversation instead of an interview.

For instance, I learned Rosemary grew up in a small village in the Appalachians before her father got a job with the railroad that brought the family to what is now Kenova.

"It's where Kentucky, Ohio, and West Virginia meet, you get it?" Rosemary asked. "Though you'd need a boat to get to the actual meeting point, but the banks were close enough for us.

"It was just after the war, you know, and we didn't know any different, my brother and me. We were the first in the family to finish high school, much less go to college.

"But back when we first got to town, it wasn't much but woods and rail lines. Ma was fine with it, being what she was used to in the hills, but as the town grew, she went more and more into herself, not really being able to adapt to the times.

"Pa had it easier, working with the yard men. He caught on as each new thing came into town and could keep us from sticking out like sore thumbs so much. Rest his soul."

Rosemary married Henry right out of college and worked as a teacher until Veronica and Michael came along.

"The two of them were more than I could handle and try to teach, even if I could've kept on working. So, I stayed at home and raised them. I'd taught elementary school, but a classroom of first graders was a lot easier than two babies at once. I swear they plotted and planned from infancy. Oh, sure, they took turns with their crying or their illnesses, but it meant we never got much rest.

"Meanwhile, Henry was working long hours with the county as a lineman. During storm season, we hardly saw him 'cept to kiss him goodnight or goodbye when he was off on the next call. But it provided a good life for us then, and when Bruce got this job down here, Henry was able to retire and the family could stay together."

"So, you had twins, Rosemary, and so did you, Maxine?" I grabbed a chance to ask while Rosemary sipped her tea. "That's a bit of a coincidence, isn't it?"

"Coincidence, nothing!" Rosemary chortled. "The women in my line have had firstborn twins as far back as we know. It's more a surprise when we don't." She cut her eyes towards Veronica, who found the fork in her hand absolutely fascinating at that moment.

"Where is Michael, then?"

Everyone but the little girls, Hailey and Bailey, looked anywhere but at me or Rosemary and kept silent for a long moment. Veronica hadn't mentioned a brother at all, much less a twin, in her emails. Had he become the black sheep? How deep did I just shove my foot in my mouth?

I was about to excuse myself for a break when Henry spoke for the first time since the introductions. "Michael went into the Army and was killed during the Gulf War. He's buried in Kenova. It was the only thing that almost had us stay up there but, well," he reached over to place his hand over Rosemary's. "We decided it was more important to be with the family we had left. Michael would have wanted it that way."

"I'm sorry for your loss."

"It was years ago, but thank you," Veronica said as Bruce rubbed circles on her back. "I know I should have told you about him, but I don't like talking about that chapter in our lives. Plus, there never seemed to be an appropriate time."

"Still, I'm sorry to have brought it up for you all."

"You didn't, girl," sniffed Rosemary. "I did. It's my own fault for bringing the room down. Of course you'd want to know where your uncle was, so no fault on you for asking."

As the older generations were still a bit shaken, I decided the let the *girl* and *uncle* parts slide, though I saw Veronica's eyes dart to her mother when she spoke.

Standing from my seat at the end of the table, I excused myself. "If it's alright, I'd like to go outside for a bit, get some air."

That seemed to break the spell hanging over the table as everyone moved from their seats to their own tasks or places in the house. Maxine put the protesting twins to bed, Veronica and Rosemary cleared the few remaining dishes from the table, and Roger, who'd been fiddling with his phone most of the evening, was down a hallway talking before I'd put my jacket on and slipped onto the porch.

I checked my phone to see messages waiting.

> WW: *Yay! Have a good time. You know they'll love you—that's what families do!*

> JD: *Glad you made it safe. Don't let them talk you into staying in MS. We need you back here in Eden Creek.*

If that didn't sum up my two closest friends in a nutshell, I didn't know what could. Windi, the eternal optimist and long-time best friend, was over the moon at me having an actual family in my life. She'd all-but adopted me back in college and never seemed to think twice about including me in her life. While I'd often felt like a hanger-on or third wheel, Windi continually reassured me to the contrary.

Jerri, on the other hand, was straight to the point and protective, which suited the small-town deputy. The idea of me being needed in Eden Creek gave my stomach the funny flips that I tried to chalk up to eating too much at dinner.

I willed myself not to read too much into the offhand statement. To Jerri, I was a good pal to hang out with. Considering we spent many of her nights off together, she clearly didn't have a lot of female friends in town, or at least one's who weren't married or had children to raise. Growing up with four sisters must make her especially lonely in the family home with only her mother for company. That was all it was. Wasn't it?

No one had followed me out of the house, so I took the chance to explore on my own. It was a gray, overcast winter day, but not exceptionally cold. A slight mist was in the air, but it wasn't exactly raining, either. More like the big old pine trees exhaling and their breath hanging in the air.

The porch seemed to wrap all the way around the house. Several rooms had doors leading out to the deck, though mine—as an interior room—was not one of them. Adirondack chairs dotted the porch. I imagined the family sitting outside when it was pleasant, enjoying the peace and quiet.

Stairs led from the back of the porch down to the cleared yard behind the house. I saw what Veronica meant about the trees seeming closer than they actually were. There was enough space for a tidy garden, bedded down for the winter. Next to it was a play area for the twins.

A path was clearly visible in a break between trees, but it was just going on dusk and I didn't want to risk getting lost. Instead, I leaned against the porch railing and listened to the quiet outside while mentally cataloging the family I was here to get to know.

Maxine, the latecomer, hadn't been as welcoming as her mother and grandmother. Then again, she was wrangling toddler twins with her husband away most of the year. That could make anyone seem cool when they were really just tired. Roger had been quiet and preoccupied. He reminded me a lot of the students that roamed campus, their eyes glued to their phones, oblivious to others around them ninety percent of the time. Seeing as he was only a year out of college himself, it tracked.

Bruce and Henry had also been quiet throughout the meal, letting Veronica and Rosemary do most of the talking. They hadn't seemed restless or bored, however. Time would tell if they became more animated as my visit progressed or if the women of their—our, I mentally corrected—line tended to choose quiet men as a rule. Maybe that's how they all got along under one roof.

Deciding I'd stalled enough and not wanting to seem rude, I reentered the house, hoping not to bring too much attention to myself.

"MC?" Veronica called softly from the kitchen. "Is that you?"

"Do you get many visitors walking in this time of night?"

She rolled her eyes and smiled.

"I see what you mean about the property being bigger than it seems."

"We lucked out with this place, that's for sure. Can I get you anything?"

"No. I'm good." I was more than full from dinner and hadn't been outside long enough or exerted myself nearly enough to be hungry again.

"Well, if you do, just let me know. We don't stand on ceremony here. When you get hungry, just help yourself to whatever's in the fridge or pantry. Plates are over here." She opened the cabinet to show me. "Right above the microwave if you need to heat anything up. There's ice in the door, here," gesturing to the refrigerator, "and all sorts of sodas and drinks in the pantry."

She opened the closet door next to the fridge to display a full, walk-in pantry lined with shelves on three sides. Cases of drinks were stacked on the floor, as were paper goods, bins labeled with flour, sugar, and rice, plus cans and boxes and packets of everything imaginable stacked on the shelves above.

"With so many of us here, we tend to buy in bulk. We just stocked up on everything last week, but if there's anything in particular you want and don't see, we can make a run to the store in the morning."

"No, really, you don't need to go to any trouble. I'm sure it's all fine." Compared to what I kept on hand in my apartment, their pantry might as well have been a grocery store.

She hesitated a moment after closing the pantry door. "Is there anything you want to ask? Now that you've met everyone and had a moment to think. Anything that you might not want to ask in front of everyone else?"

Yes and no. I wondered about the twin thing, and why she hadn't mentioned it before. Maybe it didn't matter. Though Rosemary certainly seemed to feel some kind of way on the subject. She hadn't mentioned anything more about the boy who'd gotten her pregnant, which I could understand with her husband sitting next to her. Wanting more time to mull it all over, I declined to ask anything and, instead, excused myself for a bit.

CHAPTER SIX

A knock on the door woke me just after eight the next morning. I was on top of the comforter, still in the clothes I'd arrived in, but my shoes were off and the quilt was spread over me.

"Good morning," Veronica said as she opened the door and peeked inside. She had a stack of towels in her hand. "I guess you were plum tuckered out yesterday. You were dead to the world when I checked on you last night.

"I figured you'd want a shower this morning, so here's some towels for you. No hurry, of course, just get up and going when you feel like it. We've got coffee going in the kitchen if you want some. Can I bring you a cup?"

"Uh, no. That's alright." I rubbed my eyes and tried to shake the fog of sleep from my mind. "A shower sounds good. I'll come get some coffee. After."

"Okay, then. You just take your time."

The shower helped immensely. As did the promised coffee once I'd gotten dressed and ventured into the main part of the house.

"Do you want anything for breakfast or are you the coffee only type?" Rosemary asked.

"Usually it's just coffee for me. I stop by the local shop on the way to work or whatever."

Roger was watching something while tapping at his laptop in the living room, Bruce and Henry sitting with him. Maxine had just brought the girls in from a walk outside and was attempting to get them interested in some quieter toys so as not to disturb the adults.

"Oh, I have something for them, if now's an okay time?"

Maxine looked up at me, surprised.

"I'll be right back," I said as I headed for the guest room and the presents I'd brought with me. When I returned, all attention was on me and the tote I was carrying. "It's not a lot. I just didn't want to show up empty-handed. I have a little something for everyone."

I gave the twins their goodies first, in little mini totes holding the stuffed toy and the coloring book. Maxine reminded them to say thank you before they headed over to the little play table in a corner of the great room to examine their loot.

Then I handed the other gifts out to the adults. Once again, Windi had taken over decorating the bottles to save the recipients the festive, if not creative, gift bags I would have opted for. She'd attached bows and frilly bits to the wine bottles and leather-looking cuffs to the necks of the bottles of spirits for the men.

As everyone examined their gifts and offered genuine-sounding thanks, Rosemary returned from wherever she'd slipped away to and waited for everyone to settle before she spoke.

"I have something for you, as well, MC." She pulled something from the pocket of the cream cardigan she wore as she sat down at the head of the table. "Come sit next to me, please. There's a bit of a story that goes along with this particular gift.

"Over the years, our family has lost touch with much of our history through moves and wars and separations. And yet, some things have remained constant. The women in our family always—" with another glance toward Veronica, "bear at least one set of twins. There is always a girl child born first, regardless of who they pair with. And the women are smart, independent, and a little feisty." She smiled at her daughter and granddaughter on the opposite side of the table from me.

"And while we have lost and gained a great many things over the years, one particular thing has been preserved." She opened her hand to reveal a thick silver coin and link chain from which hung a silver pendant.

Maxine gasped.

"We have passed this necklace down to the eldest daughter upon her twentieth birthday for more generations than I can recall. I'd feared, for some time, that the tradition might have to break when Veronica gave up her firstborn. But now that you've returned to us, I can give it to you where it belongs."

She took my hand and laid the necklace in my palm. It was still warm from her own. I was shocked. I mean, yes, technically I'm the eldest child of Veronica, so I suppose this is some sort of birthright, but I barely knew these people. Receiving a family heirloom seemed like a big jump from being strangers less than twenty-four hours ago.

The scrape of a chair disturbed whatever other thoughts were ricocheting around my head as Maxine, silent and thin-lipped, pushed away from the table and stalked towards her room. It only took a moment to realize why she would be upset.

Veronica's forehead scrunched as she looked from me to Maxine's retreating figure. Would she stay with the prodigal eldest and explain or go after the younger sister who she'd spent a lifetime with? She opted for door number two, and I couldn't blame her. After all, what could she say to me? What could I say to either of them?

The men took this opportunity to vacate the immediate area as well, leaving Rosemary and me alone at the table.

"Don't worry about that. Maxine has been wanting this necklace since she was a little girl and never understood why she wasn't given it when she turned twenty. Since Veronica opted not to mention her earlier pregnancy to them, it's been a bone of contention anytime talk of the necklace came up."

"But why didn't you give it to Veronica when she turned twenty?" At least I presumed she hadn't, since Veronica wasn't the one offering the necklace to me.

"And old woman's prerogative," she said with a shrug and half a grin. "Your mother, Veronica, slipped away in the night when you came into the world. We never knew and she wouldn't say what all had happened. Had she had twins, as is customary for our line? Had the first-born been a girl? Had something… unfortunate happened? We never knew."

Rosemary blinked back tears and straightened her shoulders. "There wasn't much I could say or do about the situation. Veronica went to college and things were strained between us. So, when she turned twenty, I withheld the necklace." She shrugged again. "It seemed appropriate at the time.

"We were, I guess you'd say, somewhat estranged for many years. At least until Michael died." She paused for a sip of coffee and made a face at finding it now cold. "Grief has a way of cutting through the bluff and bluster, and we reconciled. But I still held onto the necklace. Part because I'm stubborn. Part because I hoped, somehow, the family could be put back together."

"Here, let me top off your coffee. Warm it up for you." I stood with both our mugs and turned away from the older woman, processing what she'd said. Or trying to.

And I'd thought yesterday had been a lot!

Returning to the table, we doctored our coffee in silence.

"Okay," I began. "Yeah. I guess I see that. But I, uh, don't ever really plan on having children, Rosemary. It's not something I've ever wanted to do, and the thought of twins running in the family strongly reinforces my decision." I shuddered to think of handling a single baby, much less two at once.

She chuckled at my words. "A disappointment, but it makes no never mind. You're still the oldest, as far as we know."

"Oh, the twin thing. As far as I remember, I was the only one left on the church steps that day. The nuns certainly didn't tell me if there were two of us."

Rosemary nodded.

"But still, if I don't have children and Maxine does, doesn't it make more sense to give it to her?"

"Nope." Well, she did say she was stubborn.

I sighed. "So now what?"

"What do you mean?"

"I don't know. It feels strange to have met you only yesterday and now be given a family heirloom." I ran the chain through my fingers. It was heavy and solid. Nothing like the thin necklaces worn today. Not that I wore much jewelry at all. "And I don't wear jewelry regularly. I'm afraid the gift is wasted on me."

"Nonsense. You are the eldest. If it's true that you will not have children of your own, then you'll pass the necklace onto Hailey when she turns twenty."

I was getting nowhere with a polite refusal. They say if you ask three times, people feel compelled to give in. Did that count for refusals, as well? If so, they'd never met Rosemary Dumacht Richardson.

I sighed in resignation. "Thank you. I'm… I don't know what I am," I admitted, "but thank you."

"You're welcome." Rosemary smiled at me. She was probably happy I'd stopped trying to come up with excuses. Old ladies liked to get their way, after all, and insisted upon it by a certain age. My… I psyched myself up. My grandmother was a formidable woman, it would seem.

Veronica returned to the table, sitting next to me this time, instead of across as before.

"Is everything okay?" I asked.

"Yes, everything's fine. That necklace has been a sore spot for her for a while. Since I never told her about you and—Well, I never talked to her or Roger about being pregnant in high school. Until your boss contacted me, that is, and we'd met. Then we had a big family meeting, and I filled in the gaps for everyone.

"Maxine took it hardest. She and I, well, we've been very close her whole life. I think I was trying to make up for giving you up as a baby by giving her as much of me as I could, even when Roger came along.

"It's like when you have a second child, the first one worries they'll be outshined by the baby. But in reverse, in this case. But she's a good person. She'll come around." Veronica smiled at me. "It's not you she's unhappy with. It's me."

All that may have been true, but it didn't help me feel any less guilt over it. After all, if I hadn't come back into the fold, so to speak, Maxine would still be in the dark and there would be no holiday dust-up at the moment. I resolved to talk to her myself, privately, and smooth things over before I returned to Eden Creek.

"I thought it might be nice to look through these albums, MC. Does that sound okay to you?" Veronica patted the stack of books she'd brought with her to the table.

"Sure." For me, it'd be more akin to going through the archival photographs and documents for Professor Dunkirk. It would take a bit to release the detachment and acknowledge the pages and pages of pictures were family.

It hadn't felt as strange as I thought it would, especially after I noticed the pendant worn by many of the women in the photos over the years. Rosemary had shared stories of her—our, I had to keep reminding myself—ancestors and more of the family history as she knew it. The stories trickled to fewer and farther between the further we went back in time in the albums until we had to rely on the handwritten names under the oldest images.

Tucked into one page was a piece of paper, delicate from age.

> *Dearest Maria,*
>
> *I hope this letter finds you much improved from the bout of influenza that you mentioned in your last letter. Charles and I were dismayed at the news and were sure to include you in our prayers most fervently ever since.*
>
> *The baby has been growing and took her first steps just last Friday. She is still cautious, but her curiosity is bound to take over before much longer. When her brother begins walking, too, I shan't know what to do to keep them out of mischief.*

The necklace arrived safely with your letter. I was most grieved you could not bring it in person, but we also understand that your frail health must take precedence over our whims. I am comforted by the thought that you, too, would have much preferred to present it in person.

At any rate, I was pleased to put it on and I admit to you a moment's vanity as I admired the way it lay upon my dress. It will be quite striking when we have our family portrait taken. The photographer is due in town within the next month. The twins will have changed so much by then.

We will be certain to send you a copy, should our paths not cross before then.
Your loving niece,
Jeannette

Back in the guest room, I examined the necklace and pendant more thoroughly. The chain was made of smooth, solid circles of silver, each about the size of a dime, alternating with smaller oval disks. The pendant was quite ornate, rectangular, with a filigree peak at the top where it met the chain. Scrolls, curls, and silver beads stood out from the surface along the perimeter with an openwork channel between the border and the center of the piece.

There was a bordered cross in the center. Flipping the pendant over, I noticed some engraving on the reverse.

I did my best to make out what it was, but could only come up with fragments.

de erhaste
se, di wir
en, unseren
 u geben
und Tlogel.

In college, I'd taken the required language credits. My minimal Spanish got a boost while living and working in South America after graduation, but languages had never been my strong suit. I could usually spot Greek and Latin well enough—working with history professors almost always entailed something in one of the two—but the bits of words I could make out didn't seem to fit that structure, either.

I hadn't been merely making excuses. I wasn't much of a jewelry wearer. I didn't even own a jewelry box! I realized I'd have to purchase something to keep this in, in order to keep it from getting lost or damaged while waiting for the twins to grow up.

Thinking of the twins, it was their mother I was more interested in at the moment.

Just after lunch, with the little girls put down for their nap, I finally had time to talk to Maxine without the others around.

"Hey, can we—"

"Cheese and crackers!" Maxine stage-whispered her shock. "Could you not sneak up on a person like that?"

"Sorry, I didn't mean to startle you."

"Well, you did. My heart's beating like a washer on spin-cycle." She held a hand up while she caught her breath before arranging her features into the blank mask she'd worn during lunch. "Now. What can I do for you?"

"I was hoping we could talk."

"Go on." She waved a hand in my general direction before crossing her arms across her chest, leaning into the corner of the kitchen counter.

"About the necklace," I began. "We both know it should have gone to you and I have no true claim on it. I didn't even know about it. And I'm not a necklace type. Especially not one like…"

"So it's not good enough for you. Is that what you're saying?"

"No. Nothing like that. It's very old-fashioned, and it's certainly pretty and well-made, but it's just not me." I extended the necklace to her in my open palm. "I want you to have it."

"Put that away and stop this," she said, darting glances over my shoulder at the rest of the house. "That's not how it works. It's not a bottle of *wine* you can re-gift if it doesn't suit. It's a family piece, handed down by family rules. You can't go breaking them, even if you are new." She turned away and started washing the girls' lunch dishes.

I picked up a cloth and dried each piece as she rinsed off the suds. She huffed.

"Even if I wanted to accept, it's not like I could go around wearing it, living here with Momma and Granny always around. It'd cause a bigger stink than I care to be in the middle of." Dishes washed, she turned to wiping down the already clean counters.

"Wear it or don't. When you leave here, that's up to you. I suggest you make a show of wearing it at least once or twice, maybe at supper time, before you leave to make the grands happy. Then, well, just keep hold of it and let us know where you are—" She looked at me sharply. "I understand you move around a lot. Hmph. That way, we know where to find you when the girls grow up.

"You might not have known about it until today, but those little girls grew up seeing the pictures, seeing their great granny wearing it, and hearing the stories that go with it. It's important to them."

She tossed the towel into a bin and stalked back to her part of the house.

CHAPTER SEVEN

"It was kind of you to make the offer."

It was my turn to be startled as I looked out the kitchen window. Roger had come up behind me as I thought over Maxine's words. "You heard all that, I take it?"

"Yeah, I was laying down on the sofa, watching the game on my phone." He held up a black smartphone, still broadcasting football coverage on the small screen. "She's a pain, sometimes, but she's my big sister, so it comes with the territory. You showing up like this," he shrugged.

"I didn't just *show up*. I was invited." His words make me feel like I was trespassing. Or increased the feeling, at any rate.

"Yeah, I get it. But now, instead of being the big sister, she's suddenly the middle child. She'll come around."

"And what about you? Any existential crisis going on?"

"Nah," he popped a chocolate-covered pecan into his mouth from the bowl on the island. "I'm still the baby of the family. And a boy. Granny doesn't put too much pressure on the men in the family, so I'm still the same as I was before." He grinned and walked back to the living room.

I grabbed my coat from the hook by the door and went out for a walk.

I allowed myself a selfish thought, wondering if any of them considered how it felt for me. Maxine changed spaces within the family she's always known, but once I return to Eden Creek, things will go back to normal for her. Mostly. I, on the other hand, was suddenly a big sister where before I'd believed myself to be an only child. Only anything. Me against the world.

Would I return to so-called normal when I went back to my little apartment above the canoe shop in Eden Creek?

I made a beeline for the path into the woods I'd spotted the night before. The sounds of small creatures skittering around making last-minute winter preparations comforted me. I passed a fallen tree that would have made a lovely thinking spot, but I pressed on, deeper into the shadows of the trees, letting my mind wander while my feet followed the trail.

I tromped on at a quick clip in a vain attempt to outpace the swirling, not altogether kind, thoughts in my head. That it had been a mistake to come here was top most. That I didn't belong came up close behind.

I'd been fine, completely fine, on my own with my handful of friends and my work. I enjoyed the freedom of being untethered and holding few long-term responsibilities to others. I didn't need a houseful of people judging my motives or a family tree of strangers to fill some hole in my life. Should I stay and place nice or leave, possibly making a scene in doing so?

"Arrgh!"

Birds bolted and squirrels scattered as I vented my frustration at the fork in the road.

No, really. The path ahead of me now veered to the left and right and choosing a direction was one decision too many.

Panting slightly, my breath visible as puffs of mist, I took one long, calming breath. Then a second. And a third. Only then did I feel less like running for the hills.

I turned back the way I'd come. Perhaps with that out of my system, I could look at things with less self-pity or self-consciousness.

Maxine's animosity, while understandable, still bothered me most of all. After all, we were both in similar situations, just opposite ends of the family seesaw. Even though I was technically the older sister, her lifetime within the family structure gave Maxine a practical seniority that my being born a few years earlier could never make up for.

Maybe the perceived difference in rank versus age made her attitude seem more childish to me?

As I walked with deliberately slower steps than I'd entered with, I fidgeted with the heavy necklace, running it through my hands. The larger, coin-like links reminded me of the nuns' rosaries clacking against their habits as they roamed the halls of the orphanage where I spent my earliest years.

They hadn't been terrible years. It was nothing like *Oliver Twist* or *Annie*. I wasn't the imaginative type like Anne Shirley, either, using fantasy as a coping mechanism. At least not directly. I wasn't mistreated. At times I might have even been loved, or what passed for it.

I didn't begrudge Veronica her freedom. Of being scared to be a mother so young. I held no animosity toward any of them, past or present. I'd come here not so much in a desire to gain a family of my own, but because Veronica asked.

My feet slowed around the bend where the natural bench lay to one side. I accepted the seat it offered. Remembering the reason I was here, and that it changed absolutely nothing about me if I didn't let it was—if not completely accurate—comforting enough to return to the house and navigate whatever came next.

Feeling infinitely more in control than when I entered the woods, I noticed what looked, at first, like a pile of clothes. I wondered if the area homeless camped here in better weather.

There was no clearing where anyone could have set up a tent that I could see, but maybe there was an opening a few steps into the brush. Any thought I'd had to search for such a hidden area went by the wayside as I realized the pile of clothes was still inhabited by their owner.

An owner whose eyes had met mine over a gas pump just the day before.

Judging by the vacant, unblinking stare, I'd say he wouldn't be talking to strangers any time soon.

CHAPTER EIGHT

I called 9-1-1, relieved to have service in these woods, before calling
Veronica to let those at the house know why emergency vehicles were about to
pull into the driveway. She waited at the house for them, but the three men—
Roger, Bruce, and Henry—insisted on joining me in the woods.

Each came armed in their own way. Henry carried a shotgun, Bruce carried a
pistol, and Roger carried his cellphone, using the flashlight app to search the
ground around us for anything noteworthy. While I suspected the police would
prefer them not contributing to or contaminating the crime scene, a part of me
was glad not to be waiting with the body alone.

"How'd you say you knew him?" an officer asked for the third time.

"I didn't. I said I *recognized* him. I don't know his name or anything about
him, other than he also stopped at the gas station just off I-55, same as I did." I
gave him my scant memory of the car the man had been driving.

"But you talked to him."

"Sort of. More like he talked to me and I brushed him off."

"And what were you doing in these woods again?"

"Taking a walk."

"And why are you in Mississippi again?" He pronounced it as if the middle part of the word was merely a suggestion. Miss'ippi.

"To visit family."

"But you hadn't been up here before? These folks have lived here more'n a decade. How come you're just now coming here to see them?"

"Because I just found out they lived here."

"Now, how exactly does that work?" His hand rested on his utility belt as he rocked back on his bootheels. An up and down glance raked over me. "Miss Veronica claims you're her daughter. How'd you not know they were here?"

"Officer, I don't see what that has to do with anything, much less how that man came to be laying on the side of the trail, no longer among the land of the living."

"Well, it has to do with the fact that there's only two strangers around. The dead man and yourself. You have to look at it from my perspective Miss," he looked at his notebook. "Barker. Some things just don't add up."

Thoughts of Mississippi's low rank among education standards came to mind, but I didn't think that would win me any points with the officer. I took a deep breath and tried to condense the story as much as possible. "I found out we were related through a DNA test. I didn't know they were my family—" I'd stopped tripping over the word at some point, I noticed. There'd be time to examine that later. "Until Veronica reached out and invited me up here to meet everyone."

"DNA test, huh? Like those things you see on tv?"

"Just like those."

"Well, don't that beat all."

The coroner, who'd been held up by a prior engagement, arrived shortly after Deputy Dimwit (ahem, Officer Dunwoody) finished questioning me. He looked over the body, made a series of notes and quiet observations to a younger man I took to be his assistant.

"Man, MC. You can't even take a vacation without stumbling over a dead body," Roger joked.

Veronica, who'd come down at some point during the proceedings, glared at her youngest. Since that hadn't come up around the family table since my arrival, she'd definitely filled them in on at least some of my time in Louisiana. While he wasn't wrong, I wished he hadn't said it loud enough for the officer to overhear.

"What's this? Have you been a suspect in a murder before?" Officer Dunwoody gave me the up and down again. "That's something you could have mentioned at the start." He reached for his cuffs.

"It's not like that," I said, taking a step back. The pine tree against my spine stalled any further retreat. "I just ended up involved in a couple of incidents in Eden Creek. I was never a suspect."

"Involved how?"

"She helped solve the cases, is what she means." Veronica interrupted as she stepped between us. "She's just too modest to say so. She has a friend in the sheriff's department, and she helped with the cases."

"A regular old Nancy Drew, huh?" He sucked at his teeth. "Well, don't get any ideas about getting *involved* with this case, missy. I don't care how they do things in Eden Creek, but we don't need help from outsiders."

Guess who's getting a lump of coal in his stocking. If Santa is fair, that is. "I have no desire to intrude," I assured him, hoping he would leave us in peace now that the body had been taken away.

"Glad to hear it." He nodded his goodbyes to the men as we all walked back up to the house. As he was getting into his vehicle, his eyes sought me out again. "Oh, and Nancy," he said with a sneer. "Don't leave town."

—

"Aren't you just the gift that keeps on giving? Not even two full days here and we've got a dead stranger in our woods," Maxine hissed. "What are the freaking odds?"

"Get this, sis," Roger added. "She knew the dead guy, too."

"Unbelievable!" Maxine flung her hands about her head before crossing them and glaring at me.

"I didn't know him. I saw him one time when I stopped for gas on my way here. That's it." If this was what having siblings was like, I could easily do without. I was already shaken up over finding the body on my walk. Recognizing him from that chance encounter only made it more unsettling. I didn't need a peanut gallery making more of it than it was.

"So you're saying death literally followed you to our doorstep? Thanks, but no thanks."

"Children," Rosemary's strident voice halted whatever the next salvo would have been. "That is enough. MC," she turned to me, "of course you're not responsible for this tragedy and no one," she shot a look at Maxine, "would truly think so. How are you holding up, hon? Do you need anything?"

"No, I'm fine. Really. It was a shock, is all."

"How many have you found? Bodies, I mean?" Roger hadn't looked at his phone in at least fifteen minutes. My entertainment value must be rising.

"This would be the first."

"But I thought Momma said—"

"I said she'd been involved in some homicide cases. Not that she was in the habit of finding bodies," Veronica said. "And I asked you not to bring it up, if you'll remember."

"But that was before. It's not like I brought it up out of the blue. The can of worms has been opened and the hook is baited. Why can't I drop the line in the water?"

Veronica pursed her lips. I wasn't any more thrilled than she was, but it wouldn't help if I pretended like there was anything to hide. So, I explained about how, while I'd seen the bodies of Mrs. Winslow and Danny Boudreaux, as they'd both died in public places with lots of people around, until today I had not actually discovered a dead body the way he was thinking.

"But did you really help solve the cases, or was that all talk, too?"

"That I did do. And landed in the hospital in one instance."

"That's so cool."

Veronica nudged her son's shoulder with her own. "Seriously?"

"What? She risked her life to catch a killer. That's the epitome of cool."

That earned a half-smile from Veronica, but only an eye roll from Maxine. Was there anything I could do to get off Maxine's naughty list? I wasn't naïve enough to shoot for the good list. I'd settle for neutral. Didn't want to be greedy.

It was Christmastime, after all.

CHAPTER NINE

We were just finishing breakfast when a knock on the door sounded. I was on my second cup of coffee after not sleeping well the night before. I kept seeing the dead man's face asking me directions to the morgue.

The officer was back for another round, it seemed, and this time he'd brought quite a few helpers.

"Morning, folks. This here's a warrant to search the house and grounds for the murder weapon in yesterday's unexplained death." He held up a folded piece of paper. "We ask that you stay here in the kitchen area and not go anywhere in the house without an officer until we've finished our search."

"Is this really necessary?" Bruce asked, taking the warrant and reading it for himself.

"Fraid so. Is anyone else on the property that's not in this room right now?"

We looked around, each doing a mental headcount. "Everyone is here, Officer," Rosemary said. "Can I get you a cup of coffee or some breakfast?"

"No, ma'am, but I appreciate the offer."

We sat there for more than two hours, listening as they searched every drawer, closet, bookcase, and cabinet for whatever it was they were looking for. I didn't want to imagine any of my newfound family members as murderers, especially since it didn't look like I'd be able to leave until this was settled. Would I make it back to Eden Creek by Christmas Eve, as I'd promised Jasmine?

One of the officers stepped into the great room and waved Dunwoody over. After a whispered conference and the transfer of something in a plastic evidence bag, the dimwit in charge sauntered over to us.

"The room down that hallway with the suitcase," he said, standing in front of me. "That your room?"

"Yes."

"And this necklace we found in said suitcase. Is it yours?" He waved the evidence bag in front of my face. Was the necklace cursed and no one mentioned it? Because there it swung in its little plastic home.

I heard a few gasps from those around me, though I didn't break eye contact to see who they came from. "Yes," I said again.

"Mary Catherine Barker, you are hereby under arrest for the murder of Duane Timothy Redfield," he recited as he took me by the arm and turned me around to cuff my wrists. He continued to recite my rights as I looked from face to face among my family. I said nothing, just concentrated on taking deep, steady breaths. I knew I was not the murderer, but none of these people knew that, or knew me well enough to give me the benefit of the doubt.

"What I want to know," Maxine said, staring daggers at me, "is whether you killed him before or after you tried to give the necklace to me."

Their shocked and confused faces were the last things I saw before I was hustled out the door.

—

"Why did you kill Mr. Redfield?"

"I didn't kill anyone." We'd been through this half a dozen times already since they sat me in this windowless room with its single table and handful of chairs.

"And yet you had the murder weapon in your possession."

I said nothing else. I didn't see how the necklace I'd only been given the previous morning could have been used as a weapon, unless the unfortunate Mr. Redfield was a werewolf or vampire. But this was not a movie or some paranormal fever dream. This was my life, and things like that didn't exist. As far as I knew.

I had decided to only answer questions of simple facts that could be verified through other means. I was holding my tongue on any questions or ideas I had, filing them away to mull over later, when I was out of this room and, most likely, in a cell. It would give me a way to pass the time, at least.

The deputy pulled a photograph from the folder in front of him. I tried not to flinch at the image of the late Mr. Redfield laid out on a steel table. "Take a good look, Miss Barker. Right here, on his neck. The marks the killer left match the chain we found in your room and left traces of silver behind. You strangled him with that chain."

He slammed his palm on the metal table. This time I flinched. "Why'd you do it?"

"I did not kill anyone."

He sat back in his chair and stared at me. "You didn't kill anyone. Okay, fine. Who were you working with, then? Mr. Redfield's a solid guy. Maybe you weren't strong enough to kill him on your own. I could see that. So, who's your partner? Who're you protecting? You tell me and maybe the judge'll go easier on you for cooperating."

I had to grudgingly admit that his logic was sound, even if he was still way off course. I had no way of knowing what happened to Mr. Redfield. Why he was in those woods. Why I was unlucky enough to have found him. Or how he could have been strangled with the necklace I'd had in my pocket. Not that the officer knew that little bit of information.

The only thing that made even a smidgen of sense was that someone had murdered him before I was given the necklace. Which would make it one of the family.

It was not a comforting thought.

"Or maybe you can explain why," he pulled another photograph out of the folder and slid it towards me, "your family's home address was in the victim's pocket?"

I stared at the photograph. Veronica's address, the same address I'd plugged into my GPS just two days prior, was printed in blocky handwriting on a torn slip of white paper. Did that mean he knew who they were? Was he coming to see one of them? If so, why?

We sat in a stalemate for some indeterminate amount of time. The room had no clock and my cell phone, along with everything else in my pockets, had been taken from me when I was processed.

The silence was finally broken, not by my interrogator, but by a knock on the door. Dunwoody stood to answer it and shared a whispered conversation with whoever was on the other side.

He came back to the table but didn't sit down. Just leaned over it with his hands braced on either side of the photographs that still sat facing me.

"Well, well, well. Aren't you a lucky lady?"

If I was lucky, I wouldn't be sitting in this room.

"Turns out your granddaddy has made some friends in high places down here." His mouth held a smirk, but his eyes didn't get the memo. "If some newcomer showed up on my door, saying she was family, I might not be so willing to believe her, much less bail her out of jail on a murder charge. But I guess some folks have more charity than sense."

He leaned in closer, mere inches from my face, and whispered to me with coffee-scented breath, "If you hurt any of those nice folks, don't think I won't be on you like a duck on a June bug. And there won't be any bailing you out, then."

He left me sitting in the spartan room for a while longer, on my own, with nothing to look at but the dark mirror in front of me. I wondered if our conversation had been recorded, and if it caught the threat he'd made at the end. It didn't matter. I didn't do anything to worry about for myself, but I was concerned for those back at the house.

Finally, I was uncuffed and led to the lobby where Bruce and Henry were waiting. They gave me back my cell phone and other belongings and then we left with far less fanfare than when I'd arrived. No one said a word until we were in the car.

"How much do I owe you for my bail?"

"Don't worry about that," Bruce answered, as he steered out of the parking lot and headed to the highway.

"But I want to pay you back. It's bad enough I've come in and disrupted your lives in general. I'm pretty sure southern hospitality does not require you to bail a near stranger out of jail."

Bruce chuckled at that. "Maybe not, but do you think Veronica would have gotten any sleep tonight if you'd had to stay there? I may not know you very well yet. And, at best, I'd be your stepfather if you'll have me. But I love my wife more than anything in this world, and her happiness means a great deal to me. Reuniting with you has made her so happy, MC." He smiled at me in the rearview mirror. "Let me do this for you both."

It was the most I'd heard him say since I'd arrived. Not just to me, but to anyone. I nodded to him, not trusting myself to speak. There was this lump in my throat I wasn't sure I could get any words passed, anyway.

—

Veronica pulled me into a bearhug as soon as we got to the house, not even waiting until we'd made it inside. "Are you okay? Did they hurt you?" She searched my face and looked at Bruce for answers.

"I'm fine. Really. Maybe a little hungry," I admitted. The questioning had lasted through lunchtime and I'd long since run through the adrenaline that had kept me going after my coffee-only breakfast wore off. My stomach rumbled loud enough for everyone on the porch to hear.

"That's easy to fix," she said, leading me inside with her arm around my shoulders and her other hand on my forearm.

Only when I was seated at the big family table did she let go of me, but not before pressing a kiss to the top of my head.

"I can't believe they had the nerve to haul you off like that, without even so much as a by your leave," she muttered as she pulled containers from the fridge. "We've been here so long, I forgot how they can be to newcomers."

"Not that they've ever accused us of murder. Just that they don't warm up to you immediately. You have to be here for a while, get involved with things. Prove you weren't going to come in and try to change things. They watch you. Not like they spy on you, but everyone seems to know everybody and everything that goes on out here, so it's easy for them to keep up.

"It's just a shame, all of this," she continued. "How does a necklace even begin to kill someone? I mean, it just doesn't make sense." She sat a plate of food in front of me with a fork already on the plate and patted my back twice to encourage me to eat.

Maxine and her daughters were absent from the table, but everyone else watched me while I ate a few bites. There went that fishbowl feeling, again. But could I blame them?

"Apparently he was strangled," I said before I took a sip of the water she'd brought me. "The marks left behind matched the size and pattern of the chain. There was even a gap in the pattern, the same size as where the pendant hung. And there were traces of silver left in the wound."

"They told you this?" Rosemary asked.

"Showed me a picture, actually." Remembering the image nearly killed my appetite, but I kept on eating. Slowly.

"Horrible," Veronica said.

"Cool," Roger added. His gruesome enthusiasm did not please his mother. She said as much.

"What? This is the most exciting thing to happen to any of us. It might be macabre, but it's still cool."

She rolled her eyes at him but said no more.

The others around the table kept their thoughts to themselves as I finished my late lunch. I wondered what they were thinking, but also didn't want to ask. I knew I didn't have anything to do with the death of Mr. Redfield. But if the family necklace was the weapon of choice, that meant someone under this roof was responsible. It was a less than comforting thought.

I excused myself and headed for the guest room. I wasn't surprised to see everything I'd brought with me removed from my bags and the dresser. I was, however, surprised to see it neatly folded and arranged, ready for me to put back where it belonged. Since I doubted the officers were that careful, I suspected Veronica had come in to put things to rights.

I laid down on the bed and called Windi, hoping she'd have a moment to talk.

"What's up, girl? How are things with the new family?"

"Is this an okay time?"

"Absolutely. You've called during the mid-afternoon lull and Suzie is picking up Jasmine from school. I can talk for a bit. Is everything okay? You sound a little down."

"Sure, things are going great. You know, except that I just got back from being bailed out of jail by my new stepfather. Of all the things I thought could happen on this trip, that wasn't one of them."

"Jail! What happened?"

I gave her the quick and dirty version of yesterday's adventure and followed up with the search, seizure, and arrest from today. "Please don't mention this to anyone," I finished. "Especially Jerri."

"But why not? I mean, of course I won't, if that's what you really want, but she might know people up there. She might be able to help."

"I just don't want to bring anyone else into it."

"Okay. If you're sure." Windi sounded anything but. "So, what are you gonna do?"

"I mean, I didn't kill him, so what can I do except hope Deputy Dimwit and crew look for the actual killer?"

"But if *you* didn't do it, but the necklace did… Doesn't that mean someone else in the house is guilty?"

It was the same conclusion I'd come to. Hearing her reach it didn't make it any less unpleasant.

"You could be staying with a cold-blooded killer, MC. You need to come home. Now."

"I'm pretty sure leaving town would be against whatever terms my bail came with. I'm stuck here until this is settled."

"Are you sure you don't want to tell Jerri? She could at least give you advice."

"That's the last thing I need. Roger let slip that I'd been involved in other investigations and the deputy was not pleased. Told me they didn't need help from outsiders."

"Ouch."

"Exactly."

"Well, you know what you have to do, then."

"Dare I ask?"

"Show him up! Whatever it takes, you do it. And call me if you need anything. I mean it. I'll get the cavalry together and we'll come to your rescue."

"Let's leave that as the last resort, okay?" The mental picture of Windi riding in on horseback to save me from Dunwoody gave me a smile, though.

"Okay. But I'm gonna pack a bag, just in case you need me to come running."

After signing off, I laid there, watching the ceiling fan whirl above me. How was I going to sort this out with no resources and no in at the sheriff's office?

I grabbed a notebook and pen from my backpack and started brainstorming everything I could remember about the scene. Thought back through anything the officers or coroner said, my brief encounter with the deceased, and even concentrated on his final photo, as disturbing as it was to remember, with the chain print embedded in his neck.

The big question was why someone would kill this man. Who was he that someone would end his life and leave him in the woods? I opened my laptop to do what I did best—research.

It felt like only a few moments before Veronica's knock on the door to announce supper took my gaze from the screen. In reality, it had been nearly three hours since I'd left the table to rest and research. While I wasn't excited about an awkward family dinner, it would be rude not to join them. I climbed off the bed and stretched my back and arms where they'd cramped from hunching over my laptop.

Veronica made shepherd's pie for dinner. It was everything you could want in the way of comfort food. I concentrated on my bowl and let the conversation swirl around me.

The twins, Hailey and Bailey, were chattering on either side of their mother, telling some story between the two of them about a big bear who went to all his friends to make soup for someone who was sick. I wasn't sure if this was their make-believe play being recited or a story they'd been read, but they were cute in the retelling, either way.

At the far end of the table, Bruce and Henry were discussing a firearm one had recently purchased for the upcoming hunting season. I tuned them out. Roger was, again, watching something on his phone, earbuds in place, while Veronica, Rosemary, and Maxine discussed plans for Christmas Eve dinner the following week.

I'd worried about dinner being awkward for nothing. These people had better things to concentrate on than me being in jail that afternoon or the man in the backyard. Not that I missed the glances from several of them as they carried on as if nothing was the matter. Were they thinking I might be a murderer? Were they watching to see if I would do anything scary or out of control? Maybe they were trying not to spook the new girl.

I sighed and returned my eyes to my plate.

"Is everything okay?" Veronica asked softly.

"As okay as it can be."

"Of course. Please don't think that what happened today changes anything. I'm still so very glad you're here and, well, if you need to stay a little longer until this all gets resolved, you don't have to worry. The guest room is yours as long as you need it."

"Thanks." I scooped the last of the seasoned beef and vegetables into my spoon. "Is everyone on the same page? I don't want to make anyone else uncomfortable." I refused to look at, much less make eye contact with the woman across from me who'd gone silent as she wiped her daughters' faces and got them ready to leave the table.

"Don't worry about anything like that. No one here thinks you're capable of killing that man." She picked up her own bowl and moved her hand toward mine. "Are you finished or would you like seconds?"

I declined another helping and sat back in my chair as she cleared the table. An awkward quiet settled over the room.

"Let me help you with the dishes," I offered. To be doing anything would be a relief rather than just sitting there.

CHAPTER TEN

As family scattered from the table, I figured it was as good a time as any to start investigating the potential suspects. I had to be careful—accusing a family member of murder was no small thing.

Leaving aside the twins and Maxine's absent husband, left Rosemary, Henry, Veronica, Bruce, Maxine, and Roger on the short list of people with knowledge of and access to the alleged murder weapon.

Since I'd seen the victim just before I arrived on Tuesday night, and I'd found him in the woods less than twenty-four hours later, that didn't leave much of a window for the murderer to strike. My research on Duane Redfield showed a man who'd been in and out of jail multiple times during his life. Had he been associated with anyone in the house? Is that why their address had been in his pocket?

I thought back over the window of time the murder must have taken place. Had anyone left the house? I realized that my early turn in that first night left ample opportunity for any of the adults to slip away. Complicating matters were the many exits from the house. Besides the front and back doors, there were half a dozen rooms that had direct access to the porch. Even if I'd been awake and watching, I'd have no way to cover all the potential points of entry and exit.

Without a motive and with six people with both means and opportunity, that meant every adult in the house remained on the list.

I jogged after Rosemary, following her down the short set of stairs beside the pantry door to the grandparents' suite.

The icy blast of wind streaming through the breezeway that divided the living spaces was positively frigid. Rosemary's heavy cardigans suddenly made sense as more than an older woman's fashion statement.

"Hey, Rosemary. Can I ask you something?"

"Of course, hon. Come on into the living room." She held the door for me to enter ahead of her. "You want some coffee or anything?"

I declined the coffee and took a seat on a smaller version of the sectional from the main house. The older woman's walls were full of framed family photographs, reminding me a little bit of Mrs. Winslow's house.

"So, then. What's on your mind? Not that I can't guess, but humor an old lady and spell it out for me."

No time like the present. "Despite the officer's convictions to the contrary, I did *not* kill that man in the woods. But I can understand why they think the necklace was the weapon—the pattern is distinct and does seem to match the picture they showed me."

Rosemary nodded but said nothing.

"So, since you only gave me the necklace yesterday morning, I have to wonder…" Could I really ask this woman what I was about to?

"Out with it."

I braced myself, like I was defending myself in the principal's office. "How was the necklace stored? Could anyone get to it? Did anyone outside of the immediate family know about it? And do you know anyone from the Redfield family?"

"Is that all?" She took a moment to organize her thoughts. "I kept it in my jewelry box. I suppose it's possible other people could get to it. It's not in a safe or anything like that.

"People we know from church have seen me in the necklace on special occasions. And, no, that name doesn't ring any bells."

"Did you have any guests over the night I arrived?"

"Just you, dear." She looked me over from the seat she'd taken in an armchair across from me. "Was that all you wanted to know?"

Was it? I could admit my one-on-one interrogation skills were less than adequate without taking a hit to my vanity. But was there anything else to ask?

"Do you think anyone here could have killed that man with your necklace?"

"No, hon, I don't. And that includes you, by the way. I don't have a single, solitary idea about the whys and hows of that man coming to be in our woods with those marks. But I don't believe any kin of mine had anything to do with it."

I sure hoped she was right.

Leaving her part of the house a few minutes later, I heard the murmur of conversation coming from around the corner on the front porch. I stepped as close as I dared to better overhear.

Eavesdropping on newfound relations, especially those that just bailed me out of jail, was not high on the guide to being a good houseguest, but needs must when you could be related to a killer.

Bruce and Henry were leaning against the porch railings, their backs to the house. As the wind whipped around me, making me regret the circumstances of my curiosity even more, a snippet of their conversation came through clearly.

"But what was he doing here?" Henry asked. "It's been at least twenty years since they stirred all that dust up. Why'd he have to turn up now, of all times? And dead, to boot."

"Don't know, Pops. Do you think we should tell the captain?"

"He already knows. How'd you think I could get her freed so quick? Nah, Cap knows what he needs to about that lot and us. If he thinks it's important, we'll know soon enough. I'm just sorry as anything, for Ronnie's sake, that this all happened when her girl was visiting for the first time."

"No kidding. Rotten time, as any."

"We should get back in before the misses start to miss us." Henry chuckled at his little joke and I scurried back towards the side entrance that would return me to the kitchen, thoughts spinning with what I'd just learned.

Henry and/or Bruce had some sort of connection to the Redfields, if not Duane directly. Twenty years ago they would have still been in West Virginia. The man I saw at the gas station didn't look all that much older than me, but I was never great at guessing ages, so I could be wrong. Still, twenty years would put him in his late teens or twenties. What could he have wanted with either man back then? He couldn't have been local, because Rosemary would have recognized the name, wouldn't she? Was she hiding something from me, too? From Veronica?

I needed more information. I knew better than to take a snippet of conversation, overheard without context, at full face value. Still, what else could that particular conversation have meant?

I gave Bruce and Henry a wider berth than normal once back in the house, sure the guilt of knowing something I wasn't supposed to was written on my face. After saying goodnight to Veronica, I escaped to the guest room to process and ponder.

The cards in my hands offered a bit of comfort at the end of a disturbing day. A comfort momentarily disrupted by the realization that the officer searching my things likely saw the cards when they found the necklace, as I'd stored them together.

Thank heaven for small favors that Dunwoody didn't see them. He'd have had a field day adding that into the questioning mix. I didn't doubt for a moment he was the sort to jump to the conclusion that tarot cards meant black magic and worse.

I shook my head to clear those thoughts and refocused on my family members and the mystery at hand. Each person received one card, lined up across the bedspread.

> Henry—The Hierophant, reversed
> Rosemary—The Tower, reversed
> Bruce—Ace of Wands, reversed
> Veronica—7 of Cups, reversed
> Maxine—The Lovers
> Roger—King of Cups, reversed

So many reversed cards took me aback. That meant lots of things being hidden or challenged or blocked in some way. That the Tower was reversed was infinitely better than upright, though. Maxine's card was the only exception. Maybe that made sense in a way. She was clearly not hiding anything or holding anything back in her treatment of me. I could respect her honesty, even if it was as comfortable as a blanket made of holly sprigs.

Starting with Henry's card, the Hierophant was considered a leader, often a religious figure. Reversed could show someone had stepped down or been removed from that leadership role or a departure from faith or tradition.

History was cluttered with stories of family heads or religious leaders committing dirty deeds in the name of what was (or believed to be) right. Thinking back to the overheard conversation, had Henry done something—or failed to do something—to protect the family? This murder, literally in his backyard, could be the price paid.

Rosemary's card—The Tower—was a card of upheaval and catastrophe. That it was reversed spoke to a controlled person or situation keeping things together. As the family matriarch, that tracked. But it was also a lot of responsibility and, as the keeper of the necklace that represented the continued family line, and with the conversation between Bruce and Henry still ringing in my ears, would Rosemary feel it was her duty to… What? Kill to keep the story straight?

My thoughts were running away from me. This wasn't some gothic tale of family dynasties with skeletons in the closet and pretenders to the throne. This was a family who came to America and spent several generations in the hill country. And while Rosemary wasn't the stereotypical little old lady grandma baking cookies and rocking on the porch, I still couldn't fathom her strangling a grown man—or anyone else—with a family heirloom.

Moving on.

Bruce's card was the reversed Ace of Wands. Wands is the fire suit. Action and energy. Aces channel the traits of the suit into its purest form. That it came up reversed could represent a blocked energy or the eventual decline that happens to anyone granted the gift of a long life. It also showed someone whose power is directed inward instead of out. It was the opposite of being the card of a killer.

The 7 of Cups for Veronica—again, reversed—was a card of the emotional water-based suit. Any time we see the cups pour out their contents can show sorrow or regret. The 7s are one of achievement, considered a holy number, a masculine energy, one of evolution and attainment. Veronica had made it more than clear that she had regretted giving me up. That we were now reunited would have made the upright 7 a card of wholeness, but Veronica was still missing something. Or was it someone?

Was her twin ever-present in her thoughts, reminding her of what she'd lost? Did his memory haunt her? Or was it the boy who got away, the other half of my genetic pedigree, that was on her mind? She and Bruce seemed happy enough. They had two children together plus grandchildren. But was there a "what if" spoiling her present in a way only she knew?

Hold the phone. A sudden, scary thought gripped me. Could the dead man be my father? Was that why Bruce and Henry had known about him? Had he come back to profess his love for Veronica only to find her married to someone else? Were the gasps at my arrest for me or for the dead man's name?

Or had I watched one too many melodramatic movies with Windi?

I'd table that train of thought until I could talk with Veronica again. Maybe I could work our talk around in that direction.

Refocusing on the rest of the cards, I was up to Maxine.

The Lovers, often thought to be the most romantic card of the deck (that would be the 2 of Cups, in my opinion), is more about a choice The Fool makes on their journey through the Major Arcana. My little sister was grappling with a choice of which path to embrace. Her emotions were heightened, but to move forward, she has to pick one or the other.

Veronica and Roger had spelled out Maxine's dilemma with me becoming a part of the family in such a sudden, surprising way. Was her choice to accept me or continue to despise me? I wasn't going to lay odds on her decision.

But the cards were supposed to reflect her position relative to the murder. In that case, what decision was she wrangling with?

Removing myself from the equation, I considered Maxine's role as a mother. How would she explain this to them—if not now, once they were older? Should she tell her husband, who was too far away to do anything to help? Would the information cause him grief or spur him to make choices that were unwise in the long run?

I vowed to cut my half-sister even more slack during the rest of my visit and moved onto the last card.

Roger had the reversed King of Cups. The suit surprised me. Roger hadn't struck me as being emotionally driven. I could have easily seen him as a Wands card, as he presents as more action-oriented. Kings are usually older figures, or at least more mature. Then again, the card was reversed, so this could be a glimpse into Roger's potential. Just as likely, maybe even more so, was that Roger lacked the emotional maturity to lead a family. That wasn't exactly surprising since he was just out of college and beginning his career.

Regarding the recently deceased, Roger's glee that I'd found a body so close to home was a bit out of step with the usual human response, wasn't it? Was this a lack of maturity or a disconnection from emotional tethers?

Could Roger have killed Duane, and to what end? Spice up the holidays? Cause a scene? Manipulate this reunion into… I couldn't think of a plausible reason. While he certainly could have lured someone here under any number of pretenses, what were the odds of bringing in someone Bruce and Henry had former dealings with?

The cards offered no easy answers that night.

CHAPTER ELEVEN

I'd slept fitfully, wondering more than once if I should have locked the guest room door or pushed the chest of drawers in front of it. While I definitely wanted to survive until morning, I wasn't quite convinced I was sharing space with a murderer. Not convinced enough to get up from my warm cocoon of blankets to move furniture in the middle of the night.

What stopped me was the realization that if someone attacked me, he or she would only draw suspicion away from me as the most convenient suspect.

Besides, the bed really was too comfortable to leave, even if I wasn't getting much in the way of quality sleep.

Eventually, I heard stirrings in the main house that told me it was okay to quit pretending to sleep and, instead, embark on another day of pretending to be a normal, well-adjusted human part of a family I'd never known. And, murder accusations aside, I realized that role wasn't quite as tough as I'd been expecting—or dreading—it to be.

Sure, the older men were keeping some secret between them. My half-sister would love nothing more than to have never known of my existence. And my baby brother could be a sociopath. Every family has its issues.

I splashed some water on my face and brushed my teeth before padding into the kitchen in socked feet in search of much-needed coffee.

"I thought we might go do some riding around today. Maybe a little shopping. How does that sound, MC?" Veronica said from across the table.

"Sure. That's fine. Do you need something specific?" Some time alone with Veronica would give me an opportunity to explore the previous night's musings. Like if they'd ever had a pet mysteriously disappear when Roger was younger.

"Nope. Just want to get out of the house for a bit and thought it might be nice to have you with me." She looked at Maxine. "You're welcome to come, too. Granny will watch the girls and you can get a bit of a break."

Scratch that. Not just the two of us. Still, this could be good for family bonding, I thought, as I remembered last night's vow to give Maxine more than the benefit of the doubt.

Maxine's lips thinned for a long moment. The idea of a few hours kid-free must have won out over her dislike of me, because she eventually nodded her agreement and went back to making sure breakfast got into Hailey and Bailey's mouths instead of on the floor.

"My goddaughter, Jasmine, used to play with her food like that, too," I said, noticing the twins walking their French toast sticks around like people. "She and her mom would come out to see me every summer and we'd spend a week together. Jazzy liked when we found food shaped like animals and would put on whole plays with them at the table."

"How old is she now?"

"Eight going on eighteen."

"That's a fun age," Veronica joined in. "Old enough to be earnest, but still young enough to be children."

"You said used to. Why don't they visit anymore?" Maxine asked.

"Because I moved to Eden Creek to be close to them." Seizing the chance of a neutral topic, I gave an abbreviated and somewhat sanitized for little ears version of Windi's kidnapping that brought me to Louisiana from Seattle. "Now we're not even two blocks away. I get to see them all the time."

"That's a lot to do for an old college roommate."

"And best friend. Windi is the closest thing to a sister I've ever had… Well, until now, I guess." I laughed nervously and reached for my coffee cup. It was empty, I realized too late, but I pretended to take a last sip to cover the awkwardness.

—

If shopping were an Olympic sport, Veronica would have made team captain.

She enjoyed hunting for a bargain and would haggle over anything, anywhere. The first encounter of the morning had me wide-eyed and speechless, but Maxine assured me I'd get used to it.

"She does this everywhere. I'm just glad she didn't get all into that couponing craze that was big a few years ago."

I looked at her with raised brows.

"Said it was too impersonal. She prefers to talk them down face to face." Maxine shrugged.

"Okay, sir. You got me. I'll take it." Veronica said to the clerk. She gave him a wide smile.

"But she's paying full price," I whispered to Maxine. "Why does she look so happy?"

"That's the thing. She almost never gets anywhere. She just likes to talk!"

I was so distracted by this change from the soft, caring guidance counselor side of Veronica that I completely forgot to ask any probing questions of mother or daughter. Both women seemed like the opposite of what I'd observed over the last three days.

Which were their real selves? Was this a forced merriment to distract us from the awful events in the woods? Or were these their true natures and what they showed at home a carefully orchestrated façade?

Their cards of emotion and choices took on new, confusing layers of possibility.

And so it went for the whole outing.

Veronica kept up a steady patter while she drove, talking mostly just to talk, it seemed, as she hopped from one subject to another. Or good-naturedly haggled with sellers at farm stands and country markets from here to who knows where.

Maxine, for her part, would feed Veronica a few words or a name, egging her on. You could have knocked me over with a feather when she shot the first of many genuine smiles my way. No mistaking it, they went all the way up to her eyes. It was almost too good to be true—this relaxed Maxine—and I didn't dare break the spell.

We didn't make it back to the big red house among the trees until well after dark.

Newly hung icicle lights shined from the eaves of the first floor as we unloaded boxes and bags from the car and headed inside. A large fire crackled in the fireplace. Roger and Bruce were watching one of the *Die Hard* movies as

Rosemary stirred a pot of something divine, if the smell was anything to judge by.

"We're home," Veronica called out as she set her packages on the bench inside the door and removed her coat. Maxine and I followed suit.

"It's about time," Rosemary said. "I was beginning to think we'd have to put out a search party for you three." She turned and gave us a once over. "No one seems maimed or unhappy, so am I to believe you three had a good time together?"

Maxine rolled her eyes as she went to hug the older woman. "Yes, Granny, we had a wonderful time. MC got to see the shopping side of Momma. It was good to let our hair down, wasn't it, MC?"

I was the proverbial reindeer in headlights.

"I think she's still in shock," she said over her shoulder as she went to go check on the girls.

"I fed them and put them to bed already. Don't you dare go waking them up.

"I'm glad to see Maxine's let down her guard around you," Rosemary said to me as Veronica put away today's purchases. "I was beginning to wonder if five days would be enough."

I didn't want to say anything to jinx the change in my half-sister's attitude toward me, but Rosemary was no fool. "Maybe it's the holidays. Hard to stay mad when everything's all Christmas cheery."

The sound of explosions came from the television, joined by appreciative bellows from Roger.

"It's not exactly Silent Night around here," Rosemary laughed. "Did y'all stop for supper?"

"No, just a late lunch."

"Well, I've got a pot of beef stew over here if you're hungry, and some fresh bread if Roger didn't hog it all."

"I left half a loaf," he called out without turning around.

"Okay then," Veronica said as the last dish was dried and put away. "Roger, will you help your dad get the decorations out of the attic, then bring in the tree from the back porch? I'll get the popcorn started, if MC will give me a hand, and Momma and Daddy can get the movie set up."

"What's going on, now?" I asked as everyone set to their tasks.

"It's time to decorate the tree and watch Christmas movies, of course."

It was only then I noticed the girls' play area no longer occupied its spot near the front windows and a red sheet was spread in its place with an empty tree stand in the middle. Blankets had been pulled out and piled on the living room sofas, and Veronica was popping popcorn in an immense metal stockpot on the stove.

"What do you need me to do?"

"Grab one of the empty plastic bins from the pantry. We'll dump the first batch of popcorn in there to string for the tree, and butter and salt the second batch for snacking during the movies."

And that's how we spent the rest of the evening, stringing popcorn garland, drinking eggnog, watching black and white Christmas movies, and decorating the large, fresh-cut tree holding pride of place in the living room.

Veronica was a themed tree sort of person. She and Windi would get along like two peas in a pod. The tree got a healthy dose of white twinkle lights, ornaments and bows of red and black plaid, and miles of popcorn garland.

"We'll string the popcorn from the trees out back the day after Christmas for the birds and squirrels to eat," she explained.

"Back when I was a girl, popcorn and folded paper ornaments were all we'd put on our trees. No lights, certainly no plastic bits and pieces. And then one of the men would chop it up for firewood after. Paper, popcorn, and all," Rosemary added. "Nothing went to waste back then."

CHAPTER TWELVE

Saturday morning came all too early after a late night of holiday cheer. Still, hearing the squeals of the little girls as they entered the great room to see it transformed with the big tree and other decorations wasn't the worst way to wake up.

Venturing out for coffee, still in sleep shorts and a t-shirt, I saw that more decorating had been done even after I went to bed. The large family table sported a black and red checked runner down its length and each chair had matching covers on the ladder backs, with the addition of white pompoms at their folded points. A centerpiece of pine boughs, pinecones, and more red and black plaid sat in the middle of it all. The dishes and coffee mugs matched the theme as well.

Christmas carols played softly over the speakers in the main part of the house and Bruce stood at the stove flipping snowman-shaped pancakes in a—what else—red and black plaid apron.

Somewhere someone had made a mint off of Veronica's fondness for red and black plaid.

I accepted an oversized, plaid, reindeer-adorned mug from Veronica filled with half coffee and half eggnog as I grabbed a seat at the table, still not fully awake enough to process the holiday overload.

"Wow, Momma, you really outdid yourself this year," Maxine said, helping her daughters into their booster seats.

"I don't know what you're talking about. It was this way when I got up," Veronica grinned. "Some little elves must have snuck in during the night to decorate." She'd come around the table to pinch the toddlers' cheeks and tickle their tummies.

I hoped Veronica had gone to the extra trouble for her granddaughters, now old enough to perhaps remember this Christmas, and not because I was here. It seemed an awful lot of trouble to go to for a visiting adult, didn't it? But I refrained from commenting, from spoiling Maxine's good mood, until a plate of snow people with bacon scarves and blueberry eyes appeared in front of me. Smaller snow people, just the size for little hands, with blueberries and bacon on the side, were served to the little girls on the other side of the table.

"This all looks and smells great, Bruce. Thank you."

"My pleasure," he said with a smile, and went back to the stove.

Veronica brought plates over for Maxine and herself and joined us at the table. The other family members were nowhere around, unless Roger was hiding in the sofas again. It was far less overwhelming with fewer people around and I felt myself truly relaxing for the first time since I'd arrived.

Henry came and sat down next to me at the table. I jumped in my seat at his sudden appearance. So much for relaxed.

He chuckled. "Did you have a good time yesterday?"

"Yes, sir."

"Good." He settled further into his seat. "Then my news should make it two in a row."

"What kind of news would that be?"

"I was talking with my friends in high places, as Dunwoody called them. Just some fellas I know from the barbershop and our Tuesday lunches out. One of them happens to work in the coroner's office."

That got my full attention.

"Dunwoody won't like to admit it, but you're in the clear. The coroner has determined that the…" he cleared his throat, "incident occurred before she gave you the necklace. The night before, in fact. And as the entire family will testify to that, you will have nothing more to worry about."

It didn't do anything to clear the other family members.

"Do you think he'll drag his feet to tell us?"

"I have it on good authority that a more subdued version of the officer in question will be here before the day is out to inform us of the news. And to return the necklace to you, where it belongs."

"It wasn't the weapon, after all? They'd seemed so sure." If the necklace was cleared, that *did* absolve the rest of the family. I was grateful I hadn't gotten around to questioning Veronica or anyone else the day before. Any accusations, real or imagined, I might have made would be tough to overlook considering this new information.

"My sources say there was no trace of it being used to do in the dearly departed. Something about cells and such."

"Speaking of the deceased," I ventured. "What do you know about him?" I'd still heard what I'd heard, after all.

Henry raised his brows at that, not missing my meaning. "Someone's been listening at keyholes."

I said nothing, merely waited.

"Whatever you think you heard is not the whole of the story. And that story is ancient history."

"Not so ancient since it landed in your backyard."

"Ancient enough. One has nothing to do with the other." He rose, patted my shoulder, and ambled back toward his and Rosemary's part of the house.

While it was, indeed, a load off my mind and it meant I could keep my promise to Jasmine to be home by Christmas Eve and put all of this behind me, I wasn't so sure Henry's ancient history didn't need to be excavated. But I'd let him keep his secrets for the time being.

They had a way of coming out. Whether you wanted them to or not.

—

As promised, the deputy arrived later that morning to give us the news. While he wasn't exactly ready to organize my fan club, he wished me a safe, and speedy, trip home.

With that drama behind us, the rest of Saturday took on a festive, Rockwell-esque flavor. Veronica pulled out the makings of Christmas cookies and we had four generations, from Rosemary to the twins, mixing, rolling, cutting, and sprinkling sugar onto cut out cookies, chocolate chip cookies, pinwheel cookies, and even some rum balls. The twins were eager to help smash up the wafer cookies for the rum balls but were a bit put out that they weren't allowed to finish them, much less taste one. At that age, it must be tough to understand that certain cookies could only be enjoyed by adults.

It was close to their nap time, anyway, so I offered to read them a story. Instead of going to their room, they wanted to bring their tiny sleeping bags out and nap under the Christmas tree. No one else objected to this plan, so we got them snuggled into their sacks and I read them the *Cajun Night Before Christmas*, one of the books Windi had sent along with me in case just such an occasion presented itself.

Despite the amount of sugar and cookie dough they'd consumed during the baking fun, they conked out before Santa had made it back out the cabin.

"You're real good with kids," Maxine said, offering me a refilled mug of eggnog-laced coffee. "Are you sure you don't plan on having any yourself?"

"Pretty sure." Usually I reference my abandoned child status when nosy folks asked about my plans to procreate, but this didn't seem the time or place. The last couple of months had made that answer even more complicated. I'd spent my entire life with one outlook. Being welcomed back into the family that I'd missed out on didn't magically change it. I was happy enough to revise my reasoning, but the answer remained the same.

"It's just never been high on my list of priorities."

"Well, too bad. Hailey and Bailey wouldn't mind some cousins."

"There's still Roger."

"True. I guess it's all on him." She laughed. "Where did the men folk get to? I figured they'd be sniffing around for handouts as soon as the first batch of cookies came out of the oven."

The male half of the family had taken the afternoon to go hunting, it turned out. They claimed not to have seen anything worth aiming at, but I suspected they were patrolling the woods behind the house more than anything.

Just because I and the necklace had been cleared, didn't erase the fact that I had found someone dead in those woods.

When they returned, the twins were finishing up their post-nap milk and cookies while Rosemary walked me through the family tree she'd been putting together over the last few years. It was the reason they were on the genealogy site and had done the DNA swabbing to begin with. The path that led us to this exact moment in time.

Despite my initial reluctance, I let Rosemary talk me into creating my own account on the site so that she could easily share the family tree and research with me. I knew Professor Dunkirk would smile like a cat that got into the cream if he found out about it, but whatever.

Thinking of him, I remembered the frame he'd gifted me. It took me a few tries to get the request started, but I finally managed to ask, "Would it be possible to take a family photo before I leave?"

I thought Veronica was going to cry, and suspect it was the reason she insisted she go "put on her face" before we did any such thing. Before long, we were all arranged in front of the Christmas tree with several cell phone cameras set up on a console table facing us, all on timers. I sat between Veronica and Rosemary, with the men standing behind us and Maxine and her girls sitting on the floor in front of us.

CHAPTER THIRTEEN

On Sunday morning, we said our goodbyes. Veronica thrust a large plastic container of cookies, fudge, and other sweets into my hands and told me not to be a stranger.

Turning onto the highway, I did my best to organize my memories of the trip. The good, the bad, and the snippy, as I thought of Maxine. We'd left things on a much better note than we began, and I wondered if the thaw would hold or if we'd have to re-acclimate each time we met.

Overall, the experience was a good one. It surprised me at how light I felt, driving away from the house among the trees—they'd laughed when I told them a friend had nicknamed it The Wilds. I also, as corny as it sounded even to myself, felt a little like I was spooling a long piece of thread between the big red house and my tiny apartment in Eden Creek.

The bad was definitely stumbling over a body in the woods. That poor man. I'd found a little about him online, and the picture it painted was not a pretty one. He'd come up in some articles about various crimes committed in Wyoming. A mugshot more-or-less confirmed I was reading about the right man, though he looked far more haggard in them than he had in death.

What he was doing in Mississippi was a mystery, but one that—I reminded myself—was someone else's to solve.

Hoping that the end of the police scrutiny meant only the usual family secrets were to blame for the cards' insights into my newfound family, I'd dealt another set of cards before turning in Saturday night.

During the drive home, I reviewed the Problem Pyramid as it had lain, spread out over the quilt on the guest bed. The same quilt that was folded up and riding shotgun next to me, under the container of cookies.

King of Rods, reversed

Ace of Swords | The Devil, reversed | Knight of Cups, reversed

9 of Rods | 2 of Cups | Ace of Pentacles | Queen of Cups, reversed

At the top of the pyramid, in the Problem position, the reversed King symbolized someone who was unstable and arrogant. He wanted a lot from life, believed he was entitled to it, but didn't actually have the power and wherewithal to achieve it on his own. With what little I knew of Duane Redfield, it painted a picture of someone who felt cheated or left out. That sense of unfairness could be what drove him to criminal activity in the first place.

The row below the problem represented the past, present, and future of the situation. The Ace in the past seemed at odds with the two other cards. It was a steady card of planning and intelligence. Then I reminded myself that a criminal isn't necessarily impetuous or ignorant. Still, something had clearly happened between then and now to have him end up dead.

The reversed Devil in the present suggested he'd been killed to remove an obstacle. Materialism was another interpretation, so perhaps Duane stole from the wrong people? Maybe it was a case of him knowing too much about the wrong things. As usual, the possibilities were endless. The insight was just as valid, though.

Considering the problem was a dead man, the future position was a little tricky. What kind of future did he have besides burial? If justice for his death was the future the reversed Knight represented, it wasn't optimistic. Instead, it showed things would stalemate and efforts to resolve the question would be empty or hollow. It could mean his murder would go unsolved.

Thank goodness the pyramid had a bottom layer that dug deeper into the foundations of the issue. The root of the problem (the 9) suggested a dogged pursuit to maintain the status quo but with an edge of fear of losing what was. The next card represented the motivation of the problem. It fit that the card in that position was from the suit of cups, or the emotional well. The motivation for the killing, the why, was deeply personal and sought to balance the scales of a partnership (the 2).

Considering the reversed Devil in the row above, I wondered if Duane could have been blackmailing someone. It would suit the personal motivation and clearing an obstacle. If that was the case, then the police should be able to figure it out. I had to squelch the immediate thought of *if they wanted to* that followed. It's not like I had any reason to doubt the officer's commitment to justice, just because he preferred to jump to the conclusion that I was the murderer because I was an outsider to the community.

The final two cards showed obstacles to solving the problem and the potential outcome. That the obstacle was another card that was usually positive was a puzzle in and of itself. The Ace of Pentacles meant a fresh start, second chances, and abundance. Had the actual killer gained so much that they would be protected from prosecution?

The outcome card was no more optimistic than the future card of the previous row. The reversed Queen was overwhelmed and unstable, disconnected from the emotions that would normally support her.

As I pulled into my parking space behind Up a Creek, I concluded things would likely get worse before they got better. At least for those involved. Which I was not, I reminded myself.

Then I did my best to put it all out of my mind, because it was Christmas Eve, and I was about to spend it with my favorite people in the world for the very first time.

—

Even though most shops in Eden Creek were closed on Sundays, Christmas Eve meant many of them had added hours for last-minute shopping and pickups.

Lucky for me, The Book Nook was one such store. I dashed in about thirty minutes before they were due to close.

"Trying for a photo-finish?" Nicki said. The sight of her decked out in full elf regalia, complete with pointed ears, had me grasping for words as if they were snowflakes.

"Any later and I'd have been giving out IOUs to my friends instead."

She smiled as she pulled a shopping bag from the shelf behind her. "Somehow those just don't seem as festive to me, no matter how nicely they're wrapped."

"Thanks a bunch for getting these in for me."

"My pleasure. More people should give books for gifts, if you ask me."

For the record, mine was not the last bag sitting on the pickups shelf and the on-street parking on Main Street was full. It seemed like many had put off their holiday shopping and the stores who'd sacrificed a bit of their Sundays were being well-appreciated.

I knew for a fact that Windi had opened Penfeathers for a couple hours that afternoon. Living above one's store might not make for the best work-life balance some days, but it could come in handy on others.

I left the shop smiling like a loon and hurried back to my apartment to wrap the gifts and get ready for dinner with my chosen family.

CHAPTER FOURTEEN

"Thank you, Cat!" Jasmine threw her arms around me in a bear hug, though her short stature made it more like a bear-cub hug. I told her as much.

"You're so silly," she said, laying across me on the floor so she could page through the book of pictures I'd given her. With the help of our neighborhood bookseller, I'd tracked down a glossy coffee-table book of cheerleaders from all eras and areas. With Jasmine's growing interest in the sport, I thought she might appreciate the pictures and find them inspirational.

I had other gifts for her, too. Smaller things I'd picked up that Windi suggested. New barrettes for her flyaway blonde hair with little cats on them, so she'd remember they were from me. A new backpack with her initials embroidered on the back. And a few age-appropriate chapter books.

For Windi, I'd concentrated on her new status as an independent woman of means and gifted her a day at a swanky spa in New Orleans with the promise that I'd take care of the shop and Jasmine while she was being pampered. Plus a good book she could read in her off hours that came highly recommended.

Windi had been more practical, considering my recent arrival in town. I couldn't believe I'd been here six months already. She'd brought out a gigantic gift bag, one of those garish plastic affairs you could wrap a bicycle in, full of colorful throw pillows and a lightweight rug for my living room. There were even some canvas prints inside, in the same color scheme.

"You need more color in your life," she said. "And this way, you don't actually have to shop for it."

I cringed at the memory. It'd been anything but fun shopping for the furniture I'd needed for the apartment. Windi had been patient with my lack of enthusiasm, but she probably didn't want a repeat of that trip, either. Her gift let her shop in peace and me not have to shop at all—definitely a win-win.

We settled in to watch Windi's favorite Christmas movie, *Meet Me In St. Louis*. Perhaps it wasn't strictly a holiday movie since it covered a full year of a family's life and included Halloween just as prominently as Christmas, but you also couldn't object to Judy Garland singing "Have Yourself a Merry Little Christmas," either.

After the movie and putting Jasmine to bed with a recitation of *'Twas the Night Before Christmas* and leaving cookies and milk out for Santa (and carrots for the reindeer), Windi and I sat in the living room with only the Christmas tree lights twinkling.

A letter had been waiting for me from Peggy, Mrs. Winslow's granddaughter, and I'd filled Windi in on the younger woman's news.

> *MC,*
>
> *Merry Christmas! I couldn't be bothered with actually sending cards this year, but I just fell in love with your stories of writing real-life letters to Windi all those years, so I thought I'd give it a try.*
>
> *The renter we thought we'd lined up for grandma's house fell through, so it's back to square one, there. Though it might be a blessing in disguise. We'll see.*
>
> *John's firm is gearing up for the upcoming tax season—definitely not my favorite time of year. Once the New Year confetti is swept away, I'll hardly see him until after Easter. And I won't even have the usual Mardi Gras parties to distract me. At least not as much.*
>
> *But that's news for another day. Yes, I'm being a bit vague there on purpose, but trust me, the nugget of news I'm holding onto is absolutely worth it! Something big is on the horizon and I promise to tell all as soon as I can.*
>
> *Holiday hugs to Jerri, Windi, and Jasmine. Please pass them along? This letter writing is harder than I thought!*
>
> *Peggy*

"What do you think that's all about?"

I laughed. "Not even remotely a clue." I dipped another carrot stick into the spinach artichoke dip Windi had brought out with the rest of the wine from dinner.

"It was sweet of her to write you, though."

"Yeah. We've kept in touch since she went back to Baton Rouge. Usually quick texts or emails, though."

"Will you write her back?"

"Of course. She went to all that effort. It's the least I can do."

"Will you tell her about the dead man in Mississippi?"

"I suppose. It'll make for an interesting read, that's for sure."

"So you'll tell Peggy, but not Jerri." Windi leveled a gaze at me over her wineglass. "What sense does that make?"

"I'll tell Jerri. Eventually." I broke eye contact with my best friend. "Probably," I muttered.

"Why don't you want to tell her?"

"I don't know. I just don't."

"Whatever. I'm glad you're back home where you belong. Tell them to come visit you next time."

"Because they'll all fit so easily in my apartment. Right."

"That's what hotels are for."

"I'll probably go up to see them in the summer. Veronica invited me back as soon as the spring semester ends. Talked about taking a driving trip up to Kenova so they could show me around where the family had lived. But we'll see."

"Sounds like it could be fun."

"Like I said, we'll see."

"Oh! Did Ginger get her retainer back?" I was grateful the parade memory surfaced, offering a much needed change of subject. Focusing on someone else's predicament was preferable to scrutinizing my own.

"As a matter of fact, she did."

Windi's email blast had done the trick, reuniting the girl and her dental appliance much to her father's relief.

"Fortunately, the guy who found it had worn one himself and knew just how much havoc a missing one could cause."

"Talk about a Christmas miracle," I laughed.

"Okay, elf. Time to bring up the gifts from downstairs." Windi stretched as she unfolded herself from the sofa.

"Yes, Ms. Claus."

—

Windi had offered me the guest room to stay over and enjoy the Christmas morning fun with Jasmine. She'd even invited me to join them at the Wilmar's for round two with Jasmine's father and grandmother and brunch afterward. I declined both, especially considering the last brunch I'd attended there. Windi's former mother-in-law was not my biggest fan.

Besides, I had my own Christmas tradition that I'd perfected over the years. After sleeping in as late as I wanted, I showered and put on my comfiest, rattiest pajamas, found whatever channel was showing the Yule Log fireplace video (or pulled it up on my laptop, in a pinch), made myself an enormous mug of half-coffee, half-eggnog, and sucked on candy canes while rereading my favorite books in bed.

I'd put my phone on silent for the day, but I made a point to check for texts or missed calls between books. During my first break, I saw a photo of Jasmine holding a giant teddy bear.

Holding was, perhaps, a generous description, as the toy was larger than she was by half. She could easily use the thing for a beanbag chair.

> WW: *Jasmine says she's going to sleep with it, but I'm afraid it'll take up more of the bed than she realizes. What do you wanna bet it ends up living in the guest room?*
>
> MC: *If it wouldn't be 1000% creepy, you could add a zipper and make it into a sleeping bag.*

Windi replied with a horror-struck emoji. I couldn't agree more.

Thoroughly ensconced in my nest of blankets, which now included Veronica's quilt, and midway through my second book of the day, I heard a knock on the door and froze. Maybe if I didn't respond, didn't move or make a sound, whoever it was would go away.

The knock sounded again, and Jerri's voice came through the door. "MC? Are you in there? I see the Jeep."

It hadn't occurred to me that Jerri would come by today. I'd assumed she would be with her family all day and then some. I looked down at my threadbare pajamas and realized I was in no shape to receive a guest.

The knocking continued.

I grabbed my robe from the back of the bathroom door and went to answer. No sense risking her breaking it down to perform a welfare check on me just because I'd decided to hermit for the day.

"Merry Christmas!"

All I could see was the medium-sized gift bag overflowing with tissue and ribbons thrust through the open doorway as soon as I'd opened it wide enough. Not Jerri or whomever else it might have been on the landing.

"Merry Christmas to you, too."

She lowered the bag and looked at me. "Oh, gosh. Are you sick? Did those relatives send you home with the flu? That's not exactly what they mean by the season of giving, you know."

"How much coffee have you had today?" I asked as I stepped away from the door to allow her to enter. "And no, I'm not sick. I'm fine."

"Only one cup. But I may have had a *few* too many pralines, divinity, and pie slices." She sat a to-go box on the bar between the kitchenette and living room before making herself comfortable on the sofa, patting the seat next to her. "If you're not sick, why are you all bundled up like that?"

I felt my face heat as I thought of how nearly see-through this particular pajama shirt was from such frequent wear. "With you pounding on the door like that, I didn't think I'd have time to put on decent clothes before you broke through."

"Oh. Right. I may have been a bit extra enthusiastic with the knocking." She looked a smidgen sheepish as she shrugged. "I want to hear all about your trip, but first open your present." She was nearly bouncing in her seat in anticipation. Sugar-high Jerri was not a side of her I'd seen before. I couldn't decide if I was amused or concerned.

Regarding the bag, I gingerly peeked into the top but nothing was visible through the mass of decorations. I handed Jerri the wrapped gift I'd picked out for her—a book of sumptuous horse photography—before unpacking whatever lay in wait.

On top was a deerstalker-style cap in a neon orange plaid. She laughed at the look I shot her, throwing her head back and scrunching her shoulders in glee at my expense. "Clever." I deadpanned.

"For our next hike."

"I hope you don't actually expect me to wear this." She didn't, did she? It was a joke, right?

"No," she giggled out. "But there is something in there I do expect you to wear."

That was ominous. I excavated another layer of tissue and tinsel before uncovering a bag of gourmet coffee beans that smelled amazing. Cinnamon and cloves and a few more spices I couldn't quite place. "Thank you, this is really nice." I meant it. I'd enjoy this coffee, for sure.

"Keep going," she urged.

Right. There was still something wearable within and we were nearing the bottom of the bag. Under yet more tissue—someone had gone a little tissue-happy when wrapping this gift—I found a small, rectangular box wrapped in red and green paper and tied with a golden bow. Jerri had stopped laughing and was looking at me expectantly.

It was heavy, so I was pretty sure it wasn't a jewelry box. I couldn't take another jewelry gift this month. Or maybe even this coming year.

Still, I carefully unwrapped the package, as if it was a bomb waiting to go off.

"Seriously?" I said when I'd uncovered enough to see what was inside.

Jerri dissolved into peals of laughter. I only sighed. It was a stun gun.

"Look. You did better with the whole Jacob thing." By better, she meant leaving it to the sheriff's department to handle instead of rushing in without thinking. "But you have a bad habit of being around the wrong people at the wrong time. I want you to stay safe."

"Uh huh. Sure." She wasn't wrong, but still. I wasn't sure whether I was flattered or insulted.

"I'd have got you a gun if I thought you'd carry it. But we'll work up to that."

I protested in earnest.

"Besides," she interrupted me before I got more than a sputtered syllable out. "That's something you really should pick out for yourself."

I muttered something about the underworld freezing over first while pretending to inspect my gift.

"It's got a USB charging port, so you can plug it into a wall outlet or your computer to keep it ready to go," she explained as she pointed to the different features. "And it's designed where you can't accidentally shock yourself, too."

"Good to know." It was not much bigger than the palm of my hand, easily concealed except for the part that slipped over my fingers. Knowing she'd make sure I had it ready for use, I leaned over and plugged it in so I wouldn't forget.

Finally, Jerri unwrapped her gift from me. "Oh, wow, this is so cool." She flipped through a few of the oversized, glossy pages. "But wait, how did you know I used to ride?"

"You mentioned it at some point, back when I first moved to town." I shrugged. "I know you don't have time to ride anymore, but I thought you might appreciate the pictures."

"I do. This is really thoughtful. Thank you." Jerri bounced in her seat as she continued to flip through the book before catching herself. "If I'm not careful, I'll zone out looking through this for hours!

"The food is from Mom. She wanted to make sure you had some leftovers. You could have come to our place for dinner. You know you're always welcome."

"I know and appreciate it, but I have my own Christmas traditions." I explained about the nest of blankets and stack of books waiting for me to return to it.

"You don't have to be alone on the holidays," she said softly. Not laughing or even looking at me for the first time since entering the apartment. Was her sugar rush wearing off?

"I know," I repeated. "But the last week was kinda people-overload for me. Today was a nice change of pace."

"Oh. I didn't realize." She shifted in her seat and looked toward the door. "I can go if…"

But I didn't want her to leave. Not yet. "No, it's okay. I don't mind that you came by."

"Good," she smiled again. "Because I want to hear all about your week at The Wilds."

CHAPTER FIFTEEN

"Arrested."

I nodded.

"Interrogated."

I nodded again.

"And you didn't call me." It wasn't a question. It was more of an accusation.

Jerri was no longer smiling, laughing, or sugar-crazed. She sat rigid across from me, arms folded tightly over her chest and eyes glaring. I was grateful we'd become friends before I'd ever run afoul of her, work-wise.

When we'd talked on Christmas day, I'd omitted the parts of my trip that had anything to do with Duane Timothy Redfield. I justified it by knowing I had nothing to do with the crime and it being an entire state away.

But today was a different story. Heading out to run an errand, I'd found my Jeep broken into and called to report it. Windi saw the sheriff's truck pull up from her windows and joined me for moral support.

She'd been thinking aloud when she asked if I thought it had anything to do with the dead man I'd found. This did not go unnoticed by Jerri, and I was now regretting those earlier omissions.

I sighed. "I knew I hadn't done anything wrong and that it'd all work out. I didn't want to worry you."

We'd decamped to my apartment once the deputy on duty had finished his report.

"And now?"

"And now what?"

"And now your vehicle is ransacked. You don't find that a bit coincidental?"

"As a matter of fact, I don't. It's Christmastime. Break-ins are higher this time of year because thieves figure there's more loot in and around cars and stuff. You probably know that better than I do."

"I'd be more inclined to believe it if, in fact, there'd been any sort of uptick in vandalism or petty theft in the last couple of weeks. But there hasn't been. In fact, we've had fewer than average incidents of that nature."

"Fewer, okay, but not none."

"Were they looking for the necklace?" Windi asked from the newly placed rug on the floor. She'd probably be pointing out how perfectly it fit the space if the air in here weren't heavier than a re-gifted fruitcake.

"The necklace?" Jerri looked from Windi back to me. "The one your grandmother gave you that caused your half-sister to pitch a fit? That necklace?"

"And the one they thought was the murder weapon," Windi added. She had been against me hiding the mess from Jerri from the start, so I wasn't too surprised she was spilling the beans so quickly.

"But was cleared," I reminded them.

"Where is the necklace now?"

"In my bedside table. I was thinking of getting a safe-deposit box to store it until the twins are old enough to have it."

"Is it valuable?"

"More sentimental than anything, I think." I retrieved it for the others to see. Windi had seen a picture, but hadn't seen it in person until now. "I mean, it's silver, and kind of heavy, but it's not like it's encrusted with jewels or anything."

I held out the chain and let the pendant hang, swinging and twirling in the air. "It's just an old-fashioned piece of jewelry. Too heavy to wear like a normal necklace, but not big enough to be one of those statement necklaces the makeover shows talk about."

"What does it say on the back?" Jerri asked. She tilted the pendant this way and that, trying to make out the letters.

"Not sure. It's a bunch of gibberish to me."

"Ooh, I love the idea that there's a secret message hidden on the necklace," Windi said.

"Watch it just say something dumb. Like thanks for always taking out the garbage," I grinned.

"Uh, engraving is expensive. And really was back then. That's why monograms were so popular. Three letters and it's done. These days it's easier and cheaper with all the machines to do it. Back then, it would have been done by hand. I'm sure the message is something sweet and meaningful."

"Rosemary grew up in the hills of Appalachia, but the necklace was older than the generations she could remember, a fact that the photo albums confirmed. She didn't know what it said, either."

"So much for a simple answer."

The more I thought about it, the more possibilities presented themselves. "Maybe the necklace came with the engraving on it? Could have been a second-hand purchase back in the day?"

"Ooh, maybe it was stolen and unlocks some deep, dark secret from history." Windi said, excited. "Maybe it's a clue to a lost treasure, even!"

"I think you've been reading too many adventure stories to Jasmine."

Everyone agreed that the safe deposit box was the correct next step. The Jeep was drivable, and the officers had finished going over it, but I was reluctant to get in it until I'd cleaned it up. Instead, we piled into Jerri's truck and headed to the Eden Creek Credit Union to get a box squared away.

I considered pre-paying for the box for eighteen years and putting the twins' names on it. That way, no matter where I was, they could access it. Windi talked me out of it.

"It's not that it's a bad idea, but eighteen years is a long time and plenty of things could happen. You might have other things you want to store in here or you might forget about it completely, and the poor thing could end up as unclaimed property some day.

"Better to at least have an annual bill to remind you it exists. Kind of a forced memory jog."

Because I'd never considered needing anything like this in my lifetime, much less someone else's, I went with what my friend suggested. She was a mom and moms knew stuff. When in doubt, trust a mom.

Sitting in the Sip & C'est, later that afternoon, Jerri's cold shoulder over my lie of omission had mostly thawed and her questions now took a more curiosity-based tack. Windi had gone to pick up Jasmine from the Wilmar compound. Her shop, like many of the smaller downtown stores, was closed today but would reopen tomorrow to kick off the post-holiday sales.

"I think you should call Veronica and tell them about the break-in."

"Why? I'm two hours away. There's no sense in worrying her."

Jerri sighed. "You just don't get it, do you?"

"What?"

"People who care about you will worry no matter what. That's what we do."

"Okay, sure, fine. But why add to that?"

"Because you have to let people in. Eventually, somewhere, you have to open up."

I didn't reply or meet her eyes. The collar around my eggnog latte was suddenly fascinating.

"I know you're used to being on your own and self-reliant. But you have a family now. And friends that care about you. You don't have to do everything on your own anymore."

Her hand nudged mine. I started.

"Maybe you should switch to decaf," she joked. I rolled my eyes and shook my head.

"Okay, I'll call Veronica."

Jerri dropped me off at my apartment before heading back to hang out with her family. She hadn't been on duty today, but the deputy who took the call about my Jeep called her as soon as he saw me. The joys of small-town life.

"Your car? Oh my, how much damage did they do? Do you need help with getting it fixed? Was anything taken?"

"No, really, it's not that. There wasn't much in there to take. Just need to replace one of the window panels and the latch on the glove compartment. I've got it."

"Well, I'm glad it wasn't worse. Still, if you need anything, all you have to do is ask."

Jerri had been right. I had family and friends that I could lean on. I wasn't sure how comfortable I was actually doing it. Maybe that would make it onto the list of new year's resolutions I never made.

"I appreciate that," I said. "How's everyone up there? No more strangers in the woods? Nothing weird happening up there?"

"No, nothing like that. It's been the usual holiday antics with the little ones around. But otherwise, it's been quiet." She didn't take the bait I'd laid to change the topic.

"Have there been a lot of break-ins in your neighborhood? You said you lived downtown. That sounds like it could be dangerous."

"No, and it's Eden Creek. It's not like we're a regular hive of scum and villainy. Downtown is only a stone's throw from the other neighborhoods.

"Besides, this isn't the first time the Jeep's been hit. People think they're an easy target because of being open a lot of times. I've never kept much of value in there overnight if I could help it."

"Maybe you should consider getting something less… breechable?"

"Never. I love my Jeep. We've been through quite a lot and she's got a lot of miles left in her."

"Sorry, dear. Didn't mean to go all 'Mom' on you."

"S'okay," I said, smiling. Sure, we were still feeling our way through the familial relationship maze, and I wondered if I would ever feel comfortable enough to call her anything other than Veronica, but the easy concern in her voice had felt, if not welcome, at least familiar.

"Yeah, well, Jerri said I should let you know about the car thing and that everything was fine. That's all I was really calling to say."

"Jerri sounds like a good person to listen to.

"Okay, then. You stay safe, now. And call if you need anything, okay? Anything at all."

CHAPTER SIXTEEN

We were sitting in the armchairs of Penfeathers between waves of post-holiday shoppers. Several groups had come in looking for thank-you cards for themselves and their children to fill out. Windi was well-stocked with various designs for this time of year and was reaping the benefits of her forethought.

She leaned forward in her chair, an eager gleam in her eyes. "Did they find the murderer yet?"

"Veronica didn't say anything about it. I figure she would have if they had solved the case."

"Do you think it was maybe him? The murderer, I mean, that broke into your Jeep?" She worried her bottom lip.

"Why would he? Aside from being the unfortunate person to stumble over the body, I had nothing to do with it. That I was a suspect probably did him a favor. Bought him time to get out of town or something."

"But you didn't see the body when you walked up the trail, only when you came back down it. He could have seen you when you were both in the woods."

"I was so distracted I wouldn't have noticed a neon Santa Claus on my way into the woods. I was oblivious."

"What if… What if he's not sure if you saw him or not?"

I hadn't thought of that. Didn't really want to, now, if I was honest. "The fact that there was no APB or sketch artist rendering of a suspect released would negate that possibility, wouldn't it?"

"Oh. Good point." Windi sat back, her shoulders relaxing a fraction. "But still, I'm worried for you."

I waved off her concern. "There's no reason to worry. It happened up there. The break-in was a coincidence. The two are *not* related."

———

While I believed what I'd said to Windi, something I'd found while researching Duane Redfield kept popping up in my head at odd times. I'd found an obituary of who I believed was his father, and there was a surviving brother listed as well. I'd meant to research him but hadn't… yet.

Vincent Redfield lived in Wyoming and was a veterinarian. It wouldn't hurt to call, would it? If for no other reason than to express condolences for his brother's death. That's plausible, right?

A chirpy feminine voice answered, "Redfield Animal Clinic, this is Wanda. How can I help you?"

"Is Dr. Redfield available?"

"Oh, no, I'm sorry. The Doc's on vacation right now. But his assistant, Amanda, is in. She's even between patients right now. I can get her for you."

"No, thank you. This was more of a personal issue. When will he be back in the office?" Had Officer Dunwoody been able to reach him? Surely they would have contacted him by cell phone or something. Maybe he hadn't let his staff know of his brother's death.

"Not for another week." Wanda's tone cooled by several degrees.

"Does he call in for messages? Could I leave one for him and maybe get him to call me before next week?"

"I can certainly take a message, but I can't guarantee he'll get it until he gets back. He's only called the once, and that was over a week ago."

I left my name and number and mentioned it had something to do with his brother and I'd appreciate a call back.

"That's the personal issue? Look, you're better off without Duane. I can tell you that right now."

"What?"

"I don't know you, but I don't need to to tell you that Duane Redfield is no good. He won't do any woman any good. And if you're calling to try and get

Vincent to help you with some mess Duane has gotten into, that ship has sailed, sank, and been broken into itty bitty bits by the sea."

"Duane's dead," I blurted. "I wasn't involved with him." Not that it mattered what this stranger thought of me, but I still didn't want her thinking I was Duane's girlfriend. Or ex-girlfriend, his status as a corpse taken into consideration.

A moment of silence filled the phone, followed by a sigh. "Well, can't say I didn't expect that to happen sooner or later. You should have said you were with the cops and I wouldn't have given you such a hard time."

"I'm not with the cops. No, I was calling because I was the one who, uh… found him."

"Oh, wow. What was that even like? Was it… Was it messy?" Now Wanda wanted to be friends?

"No. It wasn't anything like that. It was just unfortunate, that's all."

"Oh. I see." Wanda's voice went back to its chilly setting. "Well, I'm sure Dr. Redfield appreciates your condolences and I'll give him your message when I next hear from him."

She saved me the trouble of saying goodbye by hanging up before I could take a breath.

I could feel miffed that she'd tried to get details from me and then took her call and went home when I wouldn't give any up, but she didn't owe me anything. I wasn't family, friend, police, or client. No harm done.

Still, if Vincent was on vacation, maybe he was the social-sharer type and I could get in touch with him that way?

It always surprised me how many people shared a first and last name. We think we're fairly individual and then find that there are a dozen or more potential us's out there to be found in the great wide digital world. It didn't take me long to figure out the one I was looking for, though. He was the spitting image of his late brother.

There was good reason for that. Vincent and Duane were twins. Identical twins.

What were the odds? I mean, I knew identical twins were rarer than fraternal in a general sense. But what are the odds of so many twins showing up at the same time? Rosemary and Veronica were each twins. Maxine's girls were twins. The dead man I'd found was a twin. Was this all too coincidental, or was it the blue car theory at work? Was I seeing twins as a more common occurrence because now, all of a sudden, twins had some bearing on my personal life where before they weren't even a blip on the radar?

Either way, it felt strange.

They say twins have a special connection. Some say it's even psychic or telepathic. That sharing a womb made them eerily attuned to each other. I was sure I'd seen reports of twins separated at birth even having matching mannerisms or habits despite never meeting and being raised in different circumstances. That was probably sensationalized from the reality of the situation, but would Vincent have felt something when Duane passed away? Did Veronica feel something when Michael died overseas?

"To what do I owe the pleasure of a second phone call in as many days?" Veronica answered. I could easily picture her smiling as she stood or sat with the phone to her ear.

"I have an awkward question to ask."

"Okay." A deep breath and the sound of a chair scraping against the wood floors followed. Mother's intuition or not, she wasn't wrong to want to have this conversation sitting down.

"When Michael died, did you feel something change in you? Before the official notification came, I mean. Did you have some sort of twin sense that something had happened?"

Veronica didn't answer for a bit. I gave her time to collect herself, knowing it was a big, out of the blue ask. "Huh. That was so not what I was expecting you to ask about," she finally said. "But, yes, I felt something had happened, though I didn't know exactly what.

"Why do you ask?"

"Duane Redfield was a twin. I tried to reach out to his brother, but his office says he's on vacation. When I realized they weren't just brothers but twins, well, I wondered if that whole thing about one twin knowing what happens to another, or feeling each other's pain, might be true."

"I see… I certainly can't speak for all twins everywhere, but from the ones I've known in our family, it tends to be true more than not. But it's different for everyone. Michael and I… We were very close growing up. We hated to be separated as kids and refused any attempts to have separate beds or rooms. Until puberty, I guess. I didn't much care for how sweaty and smelly Michael was around that time, so we got used to spending at least some time apart." Veronica chuckled at the memory.

"Hailey and Bailey are like that, too. I'm sure they'll squabble as they get older, but for now, they want to be with each other and do the same things all the time."

"So even if no one's been able to get ahold of him, Vincent might already know something's wrong with Duane?"

"It's possible. But, honey, why does it matter so much to you?"

"I'm not sure. My mind just keeps turning it over." Time for a change of subject. "What was it you thought I was going to ask?"

"Oh, that." Veronica laughed again. "I thought you were finally going to ask about your father."

"Right. I mean, you never told your own parents or your husband, so I figured you had your reasons. You'll tell me when you think I need to know or you're comfortable with it, right?"

"It's just… He never knew I was pregnant. I never told him about you, just the way I never told anyone about him. After all these years, what right do I have to change his life like that?

"It was different for me. I knew you were out there, somewhere, and I hoped you were well taken care of. But he has no clue."

"I get it. I mean, I think I do, at least." I thought for a moment. "Do you know where he is? Have you ever looked him up online or anything to see how he's doing? A little friendly social stalking?"

"Well, uh… Yes," she confessed. "I have looked him up. From what I can tell, he's happy and healthy."

"That's a relief."

"How so?"

"For a moment I thought — I know it's silly and all, but there was a part of me afraid that *he* might have been my father."

"Mary Catherine! How could you think such a thing? Talk about robbing the cradle!"

"I know. I know." I leaned back along the length of the sofa, flinging my arm over my eyes. Thank goodness I hadn't spilled any of my other wilder, scarier theories. "I blame it on stress and too much eggnog."

"Hmm. It was a stressful time, I'll grant you that. But really."

I was almost sure I heard a smile in her tone. At least I hoped I did.

"Was there anything else you needed?"

"Nope. You've assuaged my current curiosities for the moment. Thank you for telling me about Michael. I know it's not a great thing to think about, but I appreciate knowing."

"Of course. You can ask me anything. Even the hard things. Maybe especially the hard things. You have a right to know."

We said our goodbyes and ended the call. I still had Vincent's social media pulled up. He wasn't an everyday poster, but he seemed to share pictures of what he was doing or where he was going. His last post had been around the time Wanda said she'd last heard from him. It was a selfie in front of the sign welcoming travelers to Oklahoma with the hashtag #familyhistoryroadtrip. He was grinning broadly, the phone in front of him reflected in his mirrored sunglasses. He looked happy.

Did he know his brother was lying dead in a morgue in Mississippi? Did he feel something when it happened?

My thoughts were getting way too morose. Time to get some fresh air and a coffee down at the Sip & C'est.

"What brings you in here this late in the evening?" Molly asked from her place behind the counter. "I'm afraid we're all out of eggnog lattes for the season."

"That's okay. I'll have a mocha instead."

She called out the order and Teddy emerged from the kitchen to make the drink, calling out a hello as he passed. We exchanged the expected pleasantries about how our holidays had gone in the time it took for my drink to be ready. Instead of moving to a table, though, I climbed up onto one of the stools at the chest-height bar.

"I heard about the break-in. That got you rattled?"

"No. Well, maybe a little. I'll feel better when the window replacement comes in."

She nodded and waited. Molly may have run a coffee shop, but she had the patient, welcoming manner of a bartender, despite her loud-patterned clothing and booming voice. Today's top was a sweatshirt printed in streaks of red, white, and gold that made her look like a frenetic candy cane.

"When I was in Mississippi…" I began.

Molly nodded. "Meeting your people, wasn't it?"

"Right. Well, while I was there, a dead man was found out behind the house."

"You're becoming a bit of a magnet for them, *cher.*"

I rolled my eyes, but smiled as I did it. "I know. And I was the one to find it and be accused of the killing."

"Clearly you proved them wrong, since you're sitting here now and not in a cell."

"More or less. I mean, I definitely didn't do it, didn't even know the guy except I'd seen him at the gas station when I got off the highway…" I told Molly the rest of the story as I sipped my mocha. The café was empty except for us. It was getting close to closing time.

"And what you gonna do about all that?"

"I haven't the foggiest idea." And that was the problem. On the one hand, it wasn't my problem to deal with. On the other hand, I couldn't seem to let it go. It was an open loop in my brain begging to be closed, but there was a missing link out there and I didn't know where to begin to search for it.

"Then you need to get one, right quick. Cause it sounds like you got a lot of sleepless nights ahead if you can't get this put to bed."

I thought about stopping by Windi's on the way home, but didn't want to risk riling up Jasmine so close to her usual bedtime. Even though it was school break, Windi still had to work the next day and I didn't want to make more work for her.

Besides, we'd already gone over everything I knew. If she'd had any thoughts on it, she would have reached out.

It wasn't until the key turned far too easily in my hand that I registered the door was already open.

CHAPTER SEVENTEEN

I pushed the door open with the key still in the lock, remembering clearly that I'd secured it when I left for the coffee shop barely an hour earlier.

No lights were on, but the glow of the porch light showed that the living room was in a far worse state than I'd left it. The sofa cushions were on the floor, the books had tumbled from the shelf. But my laptop was still on the coffee table, and the television still stood on the entertainment center. Either it'd been an incredibly localized tornado or someone had been looking for something.

The slam of a car door shook me out of my stupor with a flinch. I flattened myself against the outside wall, trying to hide from the glow of the porch light. A delayed fear response kicked in as I realized the human tornado could still be around.

"MC? Is that you?"

I relaxed a fraction. "Wait there, I'll come down." I hustled back down the steps to meet Jerri next to the gate leading to the parking area and service road.

"I think someone was in my apartment."

"You think, or you know?"

"I may not be the best housekeeper, but I know I locked the door when I left and I know I didn't throw books and cushions all over the place."

Jerri swore and reached for her cellphone, calling the deputy on duty.

"We'll wait here for Bobby and then we'll make sure there's no one still inside before you come up and tell us what's missing." She shifted from professional mode to friend mode, putting her arm around my shoulder. "Are you okay?"

I nodded. It was tough to find my voice for a moment. Her arm around me felt so strong and comforting that I wanted to lean into her.

"Just rattled. I was only gone for an hour at most. Just down to the Sip & C'est and back. Coffee and a chat. I could see my laptop and tv from the door, so maybe an animal got in or something?"

Jerri took a deep breath beside me. "That means they were looking for something specific. And likely watching your apartment."

I shivered when she removed her arm from my shoulders and scoped out the surrounding area, and it wasn't only from the lack of her warmth. What she'd said made sense, more sense than I wanted to believe in that moment. Someone had been watching the apartment. Waiting for me to be gone before they broke in. What were they after? I didn't own anything of value.

Deputy Jones, Bobby to his friends, arrived and pronounced the area safe to enter. The apartment might be clear of boogeymen, but no mere declaration could clear the chaos before us.

They hadn't merely tumbled the cushions from their spots, they had sliced them open. Same for my mattress and pillows in the bedroom. They'd tossed my clothes everywhere, emptied the medicine cabinet onto the floor, and the kitchen cupboards, what few there were, had been ransacked.

"I understand it might be hard to tell with everything in such a state, Ms. Barker, but does anything look like it's missing?"

"Please, call me MC. And, no, everything seems to be here." If anything, having my worldly possessions strewn about the place made it easier to see that everything was, in fact, present and accounted for.

"Well, if something turns up missing as you start putting things away, you can let us know and we'll make a record of it." He flipped a page in the notebook he held. "Can you think of anything the thieves might have been looking for? Do you keep cash or jewelry in the home?"

"No. Nothing like that." Jewelry made me think of the necklace and I shot a glance to Jerri, who was standing behind the deputy watching over his shoulder as he made his notes. Her eyes met mine with a quirked brow.

Okay, fine. This could, maybe, have something to do with the necklace and possibly even the incident in Mississippi. But why? How were they connected? And how had I found myself in the middle of another murder investigation?

"You're going to want to have your lock changed. It's not damaged, but I can see where it was jimmied. Maybe talk to your landlord about putting a stronger lock in its place, or an extra deadbolt. If you come by the station tomorrow, we can give you a copy of the official report to file with your insurance to help with repairs and replacements."

The deputy left us standing in the wreckage that was my living room.

"Grab a few things for tonight. I already called Windi and let her know you were on your way over."

"I wish you wouldn't have bothered her. I've stayed in worse places." I hadn't, really. But aside from the mess that could be cleaned up easily enough, it wasn't that bad.

"You're not staying here until we get those locks changed and reinforced. Grab your toothbrush and let's go."

I sighed and waded through the clutter toward the bathroom, trying to locate said toothbrush. Jerri followed.

"On second thought, just grab some clothes. I'll drop you off at Windi's and then run to the drugstore for whatever you need. No telling whose hands might have been on it, right?"

I hadn't thought it about like that. In fact, I hadn't thought much beyond what was or wasn't missing. Not who might have been in here or what they might have touched. Gooseflesh prickled my arms. I was suddenly glad that I didn't have to stay here tonight. Glad that I wouldn't be alone, either.

Jerri's arm was once again around my shoulders, her free hand rubbing my arm. I hadn't noticed I was trembling until someone steady was next to me. I was both embarrassed and grateful for the attention.

"I'd say the initial shock has worn off, and it's all starting to sink in. Am I right?" Jerri alternated between rubbing my arms and back.

"S-something like that." My teeth chattered when I tried to speak and wouldn't stop.

She walked me out of the bedroom, sat me on a bar stool, and wrapped a blanket around my shoulders. "Sit tight, I'll grab your gear, and we'll get out of here."

"Drink this." Windi pressed a steaming mug of hot chocolate into my hands. The first sip made me cough. It was spiked. "I figured a little something extra wouldn't hurt after finding your apartment like that."

Jerri had already gone to fetch the aforementioned toothbrush, leaving me in the capable hands of my best friend, who thought I might need alcohol to make it through the evening. I shrugged, taking a second, careful, sip. What could it hurt?

"The guest room is ready for you and you can stay as long as you need. Don't think you have to get everything back to normal in one day, okay?" She sat next to me on the sofa and leaned over to give me a hug.

We sat that way, neither speaking, until Jerri returned fifteen minutes later. I was halfway through the extra-large mug of cocoa and getting drowsy. My eyelids were only half open, but I didn't want to move from this spot. Didn't want to break the spell. Didn't want to face the reason I was sitting in my friend's living room instead of my own.

Jerri let herself in, sat a bag containing more than just a toothbrush on the coffee table, and smirked our way. I almost thought she was making fun of me until she reached over and nudged Windi gently, waking her up. I guess I wasn't the only one comfortable in this spot.

"Oh, gosh. Sorry about that," she blushed. "Long day."

And there it was. The guilt returned for disrupting her quiet evening with another fine mess.

"Let's let you both get to bed, then." Jerri took the cocoa from me and gave it a whiff. "I see." She arched a brow in Windi's direction.

"Just something to settle her nerves."

"I'm right here," I finally spoke. I was still swaddled in the blanket from my apartment and feeling somewhat toasty both inside and out.

"Of course you are," Windi cooed and patted my shoulder.

I felt like a child being talked over and around. Whatever. I was too tired to truly get angry about it. Instead, I let them lead me to the guest room, my eyes mostly closed as someone slipped off my shoes and tipped me over onto soft pillows. I felt the weight of another blanket settle over me and then nothing more.

CHAPTER EIGHTEEN

"No fair!"

The indignant voice of my goddaughter woke me the next morning. As the events of last night shuffled to the top of my memory, I wanted nothing more than to burrow into the nest of blankets and forget for just a few moments more.

It was no use.

"Y'all had a sleepover and didn't tell me."

"It's not like that, Jasmine. Please keep your voice down or you'll wake her up."

"Too late," I said as I rounded the corner. "I'm up."

Jasmine looked sheepish for a fraction of a second before she hopped off her stool, hurried over, and hugged my waist. "Sorry for waking you up."

"It's okay," I assured her as I patted her head and shuffled us toward the breakfast bar where Windi was holding out a cup of coffee for me.

"Why'd you stay here last night and not wake me up?" Jasmine finally let go of my waist and went back to eating her breakfast.

I looked at Windi. Did we want to tell Jasmine that someone had broken into my apartment? Would that scare her?

"Something broke at her place, so she ended up coming over late at night. You were already asleep, and we went straight to bed, too."

Nicely done.

"What broke?"

"The door—"

"The lock—"

"The bed—"

We all spoke at once and stopped just as fast. Jerri was the first to recover.

"The lock on MC's door is messed up and something got in and made a big mess that was too much to clean up last night."

"What messed up the door?"

"Not sure," I answered. "But we'll get it fixed today and I'll get the mess cleaned up and that'll be it. No big deal."

"And if it takes longer than today to get it fixed, MC can stay here again if she needs to, right?" Windi looked from me to her daughter and back.

"Is it bad that I hope it doesn't get fixed today?"

Ah, the honesty of a child.

"Not bad," I told her. "But I have to get my door fixed so everything stays safe."

Fortunately, she took that as her answer and finished her breakfast. Soon enough, she was back in her room getting dressed for the day.

"You came back awfully early," I said to Jerri.

"Never left."

I looked from her to where she gestured to the couch. There was a pillow and blanket stacked neatly on one seat. It took a minute to realize she, like me, was in the same clothes she was wearing last night. "You didn't have to do that."

"Mom's got a houseful, still, and there's no way I was leaving you unprotected. Remember that all happened during the hour you were out of the apartment, after they'd already searched your vehicle. I didn't want to take the chance they were still watching you and would choose a more direct route next."

Her words sent a chill down my spine. I was less eager to get my apartment back or to leave the safety of our little crowd here at Windi's.

"Before you stay at the apartment again, we not only need to get the lock upgraded but also install a security system. I'll work it out with Roscoe if he says anything, but I don't think he will. I've suggested Windi put in a security system here as well."

"And I'm going to take that advice," she said.

"I have one in the store, but didn't really worry about one here on the upper floors." The residential entrance was inside a small vestibule inside the back door of Penfeathers. Realistically, someone would have to get past it to enter, but the alarm was off during business hours. "Now I'm rethinking that choice."

"Good." Jerri finished her coffee and set the mug in the sink before grabbing her keys from the counter. "I need to run by the station and adjust my schedule for the day — Family emergency," she said as I opened my mouth to protest. "I'll pick up a copy of the report from last night if it's ready while I'm there."

—

I'd returned to the apartment armed with a box of garbage bags. Anything not worth fixing or saving went into one. There'd been far more miscellaneous papers strewn about than I'd realized I'd owned. Most were copies of notes from different research projects, some junk mail I hadn't yet gotten rid of, and a few newspapers waiting to be recycled. Why had they felt the need to toss the newspaper around sheet by sheet?

The dry food in the kitchen that had been dumped out got swept up and tossed. I observed a moment of silence for the bag of gourmet coffee beans I'd been gifted but not yet had a chance to try. My shopping list was growing longer by the minute.

Toiletries in the bathroom were next. Mostly drugstore varieties. Easily replaced. I was surprised to find the remains of the pain pills I'd been prescribed after my run-in with Margaret Hanover were still there. Knocked to the ground, yes, but easily spotted in their amber plastic pill bottle.

It only brought home the fact that this was not a typical break-in.

Sounds from the front door startled me, but I crept towards the bedroom door, despite my fear.

"It's just me," Mr. Roscoe called out, settling my nerves. "Came to take a look at this door of yours."

He looked around the disheveled sofa and the pouf spilling stuffing out onto the living room rug. "They sure did a number in here, didn't they?" He tch'd under his breath and muttered something about hooligans as he bent to inspect the lock.

"They didn't do any damage that I can see, but I can surely understand you wanting to change the lock."

"And maybe adding a second lock too? And a sliding chain inside?"

"Sure, we can do that." He set to work, taking measurements for the new deadbolt and strike plate.

"Deputy said they didn't take anything. What do you s'pose they were looking for?"

"Haven't a clue. What you see is what I've got."

"Hooligans making trouble." He shook his head and returned to his work for a few minutes more before leaving to pick up the necessary supplies.

I'd lived in some pretty shady places over the years, places where three deadbolts on the door was a minimum offering. I'd had the Jeep broken into a few times in the early days, but never the apartment I was living in. Of all those places I'd been, it seemed odd that sleepy little Eden Creek would be the first.

Steve, the same installer who'd helped Peggy after her grandmother's home was ransacked, showed up not five minutes after Roscoe departed. He was a short, slightly bow-legged country boy. A man of few words, he worked in silence. I suspected he was listening to some sports show or game through the bud secured in his left ear.

While he worked, I trekked out to the nearest big box store to restock on the items I'd need sooner than later. Even though I was still waiting on the window replacement and the chill wind bit at me through my long-sleeved shirt and windbreaker, it was worth the trip to clear my head of the chaos that reigned in the apartment. Especially when I knew someone would be there, someone I trusted, while I was away.

"That ought to do you for, Ms. MC," Steve said, climbing down his ladder after affixing the final motion sensor when I returned, arms laden with bags. "You remember how the panel works and all, right?"

I assured him I did, and he walked me through how to disable the sensors if I wanted to open a window for some reason.

As if choreographed, Roscoe returned as Steve left and set to installing the new hardware. His power tools made a comforting racket as I unpacked my replacement groceries. I wasn't one for post-holiday shopping—I preferred to avoid the crowds at all costs—but I couldn't argue with the convenience of so many things being on sale when unexpected replacements were required.

I was just switching the non-ruined set of sheets from the washer to the dryer when Jerri arrived with a steaming-hot pizza from Bubba's. The growling of my stomach reminded me I hadn't eaten lunch.

"Figured you could use a break when you weren't at Windi's. You didn't text me back, either. Have you been at it all day?"

"Pretty much." I retrieved my phone from the bedside table and saw three missed texts. One from Windi, two from Jerri. "Sorry about that."

Jerri sat the pizza on the coffee table, grabbed some bottled waters from the fridge, and helped me arrange the sofa cushions to their least damaged sides. Completely at home in my space, she fetched a blanket from the bedroom closet and draped it over the sofa, hiding the rest of the damage.

"Not exactly good as new, but maybe out of sight, out of mind for a while." She gestured to her handiwork. "Come. Sit. Eat."

I did as I was told. When I didn't say anything, just dove in for my first slice of Bubba's everything pizza, Jerri grabbed the remote and cued up the next episode of *NCIS*. By the end of a second episode, the pizza was finished and so was I. Being still after such a busy day had my eyelids drifting closed without my permission.

Aside from commenting on some of the on-screen antics, Jerri had let me be and not pushed for conversation. But I could feel her eyes on me periodically. Watching me. Checking on me.

"You want me to drop you at Windi's?"

"No. I'm staying here. The locks are new. The alarm is set. I'm safe as houses."

CHAPTER NINETEEN

The moment my head hit the pillow, my eyes popped open. I was bone-weary and mentally exhausted, yet sleep refused to come. It could have been that the pillows were new and therefore not broken in. Or that I was so attuned to my mattress that I could feel the tear on the side that was now face-down on the box spring. The princess and the pea I was not. Or never had been, seeing as I'd always been able to sleep wherever I was, no matter the condition of the sleep surface.

It could be anything, as long as it wasn't that each and every night sound had me freezing stock-still and listening for footsteps on the landing or the jiggle of the door handle.

By three in the morning, I finally gave up, got up, and went into the living room to find something to watch on television until the rest of the world woke up. Campus was still closed for the holidays, so I had plenty of time to reset my sleep schedule. Later. When things went back to normal.

I fired up the espresso machine not because I needed the energy, but more for the ritual and warmth of it all. I felt a momentary pang that I was not digging into the bag of gourmet beans Jerri had gifted me. The replacement bag

I'd ordered would be here in a few days. Until then, the supermarket brands would have to do.

Giant travel mug of coffee in hand, I browsed the streaming options for anything to take my mind off the fact that it was oh-dark-thirty in the morning and I was killing time until I was "allowed" to be awake and active. Whatever that meant.

I was definitely not in the mood for the holiday schlock-fest of sweet romances and second chances that were still abundant on every network. Instead, I scrolled through lists of documentaries, searching for something that hit the mark.

While a 'where are they now'-style program reviewed the post-limelight days of 80s hair bands, I gave in and looked at what I knew so far.

A man had been murdered and dumped behind the house I was visiting out of town.

I'd been given a necklace that had been in our family for umpteen generations, which both did and didn't match the suspected murder weapon.

My vehicle and apartment had been broken into and nothing removed from either one.

The necklace was the only item I owned that was stored off-site. In a safe deposit box at the local credit union.

What was the connection? At this point, I'd be foolish to insist that it was all a coincidence.

I opened my laptop to see if I could find out anything more about the dead man or his family and froze.

The Notepad app was open. It was not blank.

You have something that belongs to me.
I will get it back.
Do not call the police or things will get worse.
Be seeing you.
Soon.

—

"Hey, Jerri, are you working today?" She'd answered my call, but that didn't mean she wasn't on duty, just that she wasn't in the middle of something important.

I'd called as soon as it was decent. Waiting one extra minute past 8 a.m. so it wouldn't seem like I was watching the clock. Because I was absolutely watching the clock.

"Yeah. I get off at three. Do you want me to come by after?"

"I do. But…" This was going to sound awkward, but I couldn't think of a better way to say it. "Can you change out of your uniform before you come over?"

There was a pause before she answered. "Sure. I can do that. Any particular reason why?"

"Yes, but I'd rather explain when you get here."

In the meantime, I called Officer Dunwoody to see if there'd been any updates on the case.

"We already cleared you. What more do you want?"

"To know the person actually responsible has been identified, apprehended, and incarcerated. If that's not too much trouble." I wasn't wholly successful in keeping the sarcasm from my tone.

"You want world peace on the side?"

I changed tactics. "It's just that since I returned to Eden Creek, I've had my Jeep and my apartment broken into. I'm concerned that it might have something to do with Mr. Redfield's murder."

"Well, now, as you've so generously pointed out, that all happened in Eden Creek. It's a bit outside of our jurisdiction." He smothered a chuckle under a cough. "Besides, aren't you all buddy buddy with the deputies there? Why aren't you bothering them instead of me?"

"They're looking into it—"

"Then I have to ask again, why are you bothering me about it?"

"The events could be connected."

"Ms. Barker. The only connection is you. And you being a lightning rod for trouble is not only not my problem, but it's not even a crime. That's just bad luck for you and anyone around you."

I waited another hour to be sure I wouldn't wake them up before I called Veronica and asked her to put herself and Rosemary on speakerphone so I could fill them in.

"Your apartment, too?" Shock was clear in Veronica's voice. "Did they take anything?"

"No, just made a big mess. I think they were looking for something, though. Like maybe the necklace?"

"You still have it, right?" Rosemary asked.

"It's in a box at the bank. Can you think of anyone who would be after it like this?"

"No. It's a family piece. It's not like we make a big show of it to other people."

"I only wore it on special occasions," Rosemary added. "It was a little fancy for everyday wear."

She wasn't wrong there. It was big and a little gaudy, even. So why did it seem to be so important to a veritable stranger?

"One other thing. Do you know what the inscription means? I could only make out bits and pieces, but I'm not even sure what language it is."

"Oh that. I've never known what it meant, really. No one in my immediate family could read it, either," the older woman chuckled. "We always figured it was a special phrase between the first two women who exchanged it. That part of the story has been lost to time."

By the time we'd finished talking, I figured it was a safe enough hour to try Wyoming once again.

"Oh. It's you." Wanda's customer service voice slipped into the register most often reserved for telemarketers and bill collectors.

"I was wondering if you'd heard from the doctor since the last time we talked. Were you able to pass on my condolences?"

"As a matter of fact, I did. Seems he's finally wised up to that brother of his because he didn't seem bothered in the least. In fact, he's decided to close the practice and retire."

"I didn't think he was retirement age."

"Age or not, he's decided to sell it all and move somewhere warmer. So there's really no reason for you to call here again."

I was still fuming over the rebuff when Jerri arrived. Out of uniform, as requested.

"I'm really looking forward to your explanation," she offered in greeting. "And what point are all these locks if you leave the door open?"

"I knew you were coming over," I shrugged. But inside I was kicking myself for not checking the locks. I knew I'd locked up last night before bed, but I had forgotten to re-secure them after I brought another bag of trash down to the dumpster a couple of hours ago. Anyone could have walked in.

I reopened the laptop and turned it her way as she took a seat on the sofa. "This is why I called you."

"When did you find this?" She was all business.

"Early this morning. First time I'd opened the laptop since the break-in." I decided not to mention the insomnia.

"You should have reported this immediately."

"I did. I called you."

"But you didn't tell me why." Her hands made a slicing motion toward the note on the screen.

"You were the one who said they were likely watching the apartment to see when I'd gone out. I figured if they were still watching, it would be better you came over in friend-mode than in cop-mode."

That earned me a sideways glance. "It's not like the two *modes*, as you put it, are mutually exclusive."

"But maybe *they* don't know that."

Jerri scrubbed her face in her hands. "Okay. Did you use the laptop after you found the note?"

I shook my head. "Once I read the message, I closed the lid until you got here. Used my phone for anything I needed to look up." I shook the phone in my right hand. I'd been fiddling with it off and on all day.

"Let me get my kit out of the back of the truck and at least check for fingerprints."

"But the note said—"

"I know what the note said. But criminals do not get to call the shots, MC. I'll be as discrete as possible so the boogieman, rougarou, or whoever it is won't see what we're up to. Give me some credit, okay?"

Her mood had not changed, nor had her voice lost its frosty edge by the time she finished dusting the laptop. "Lock up after me," she reminded as she left. "And maybe consider going back to Windi's for a few more nights."

Feeling a bit chastised, I set to securing the door behind Jerri when I heard Mr. Roscoe wishing a customer a Happy New Year from downstairs. I reopened the door and waved down from the landing to my landlord.

"Happy almost New Year, Mr. Roscoe."

"Hello, trouble," Mr. Roscoe grinned up at me from the base of the stairs. "You sure have kept things interesting 'round here."

"About that," I began. "I just wanted to thank you, again, for getting the locks fixed."

"No problem. But how's about you make a resolution to not do whatever it is you did to have such bad luck, huh?"

"Oh. Right. I'll get on that." Not at all sure how I was supposed to avoid trouble when I hadn't a clue how I'd attracted it to begin with.

Back inside, I went to make a sandwich for supper but couldn't find the mayo. I looked in the cupboards and checked for any unpacked shopping bags. Even fished the receipt out of the trash can to confirm that I hadn't bought it during my errands. It made for a dry supper, but a couple of bottles of water washed it down.

How I still had energy after the previous day and night, I had no clue. But I did. I was wired for sound and unsure of what to do with myself. It was the first time I missed the easy access to the Wilmar's pool. Swimming laps, even in winter, would have been a tremendous stress-reliever.

Pacing to work off some of my excess energy, I tripped on the edge of the blanket covering the sofa damage and landed hard in the small aisle between sofa and coffee table. Flexing my wrists, sore from stopping my fall, I turned my head and saw yet another piece of fluff spilling from the damaged furniture. One more polyfil tumbleweed showing just how mucked up my life had become.

Pulling myself up to sitting, I looked at the bit of fluff in my hands, pulling it apart with my fingers. In the quiet of the apartment I felt the weight of it all come crashing down on me. They say it takes only a final straw to break a camel's back. This bit of fluff was that proverbial straw. It was the last thing on top of rude people on the phone, the teasing of my landlord, and being treated like a child by someone who I was finally realizing I cared about as more than a friend.

I felt the unfamiliar sting of tears rush my eyes and, before I knew it, I was sobbing against the mangled sofa.

CHAPTER TWENTY

The next morning I woke wedged between the coffee table and the sofa. Eyes gritty, back aching from the awkward position, and butt numb. But at least I'd slept.

I'd never been much of a crier. A school guidance counselor once tried to tell me it was good to let emotions out from time to time, but it wasn't something I'd ever been comfortable with. Still, a part of me felt a little lighter after the tears. After all, I couldn't get much lower, could I?

After a shower, a change of clothes, and swigging down some pain killers with a large mug of coffee, I gave myself a pep talk for how the rest of the day would go.

Things may look bleak at the moment, but that's all it was. A moment. I was done feeling sorry for myself and wallowing. It was time to figure out what I could do to change things. And the thing I could always do was research.

Fortified and with a renewed sense of purpose, I opened my laptop to begin. Only to cringe back from the keys that were gritty with the remains of fingerprint powder. Ugh.

I thought back to my first few weeks of traveling after college…

Windi,

You know when you tried to talk me out of joining the Peace Corps? With all the arguments you offered, you neglected the one thing that might have swayed me towards grad school over South America: the dirt.

There is grit everywhere. Not just on my skin, which is bad enough, but in my hair, in my sinuses, and even the crunch of it in my teeth. Grit is probably my least favorite sensation in all the worlds (which you probably remember from that one spring break in Panama City).

Oh, well, a little grit isn't the worst thing. After all, we're down here to do some good for these villages, and they live with this their entire lives. I can endure it for two years. Besides, you have often said I need some of my rough edges softened. Maybe the grit will act like a pumice stone on my life.

MC

I still hadn't made peace with gritty textures, be it sand or whatever horrific material fingerprint powder was made from. I brushed what I could from my fingertips and keyboard with paper towels, but felt like I wanted nothing more than another shower to rinse off the finer particles.

Which was worse, I asked myself. Home invasion or powdery infiltration?

At that moment, I honestly couldn't decide.

A perk of just putting everything back where it belonged was that I knew exactly where the mini vacuum for electronics was. I took care of the grit and settled for a thorough scrubbing of hands over a second shower. I recentered my focus on what connected the dead man to me.

Using the father's obituary as my guide, I drew the barest branches of their family tree and set about searching for those names on the genealogy site.

It was slow, painstaking work going through archived documents of people I did not know and only had the barest of information on. I didn't even know if this was the right trail to follow. I reasoned, if reason came into it at all, that if whomever killed Duane Redfield was after the necklace, and the necklace had been in Rosemary's family for generations, that somewhere their paths must have crossed, right?

Add to that the home address found in his pocket. That suggested he was looking for us—or them—for some reason. Since he, she, or they were now coming after me, it had to be something that started there and ended up here that drew them. That left the necklace. Or the quilt that Veronica made for me.

Speaking of the quilt —

I shot up from the sofa and searched the bedroom for the quilt, wracking my brain to remember the last time I'd seen it. Christmas, in my nest of blankets. I rifled through the remaining linens and clothes piled up waiting to be washed, but it wasn't there.

A fist curled inside my chest. My breathing became shallow. Eyes stung for another round of tears. Was this what a panic attack felt like? Over a quilt? I felt like I was well and truly falling apart, becoming this emotional twice in as many days. This was definitely not like me at all and I couldn't say it was a welcome change in any way, shape, or form.

I paced between the two main spaces of the apartment, concentrating on my breathing and my footsteps, getting the two in sync—four steps for each inhale or exhale—before picking up the phone to call Jerri.

"I found something missing," I said, skipping hello. My voice sounded mostly calm.

"Wanna run that by me again?"

"The quilt Veronica made me. I just noticed it was missing. I can't find it anywhere. I don't know why they would take, but it's not here."

"It's okay, the quilt isn't missing."

"But it's not here."

"Yes, I know, but listen to me for a second. I have the quilt."

"You do? But why?" Why would Jerri have taken my quilt? What sense did that make? I sank down onto the couch, adrenaline rush colliding with the brick wall of confusion, leaving me weak.

"Listening, remember?" She sighed. "I brought it to Mom to fix when I noticed it got slashed with the other sheets and stuff on your bed. I was hoping to have it back before you noticed it was gone."

"Oh."

"I'm sorry. I should have told you, probably, but it seemed like a simple thing to fix. In fact, it's done. I just haven't gotten back to your place to sneak it in somehow."

"Oh." I seemed to have lost whatever part of the brain that handled intelligent speech. That was sweet of her. She had no way of knowing it'd send me into full-on panic mode. "Well, now you don't have to sneak. And thank you for having it fixed."

"Sure. No problem. Mom was happy to do it."

"I'll make sure to thank her next time I see her."

I was still sitting on the sofa, staring off into nothingness, when my phone rang, effectively hitting play on my activity controller once again.

"Mary Catherine, what are you doing working when you're supposed to be enjoying the holiday fun? I'm not some slave-driver, you know."

"Professor Dunkirk?"

"Of course it's me. Who else would it be?"

"Right. But what do you mean? I'm not working."

"Oh, so are you doing some personal research, then?"

"What?" A glance at the laptop screen showed I'd logged in under the college account and not my own, newer one. He'd probably gotten a message about the login onto the genealogy database when I started researching the Redfields. "Well, sort of…"

"That's splendid! I'm so happy to see your interest piqued! Tell me, is there anything I can do to help? Was your visit with your family that successful, then?"

"It's complicated."

"Families always are," he laughed. "Don't tell me they have you off looking for someone famous in their lineage or anything like that."

"Not exactly." I gave him the nickel version of the last week and a bit and what led me to research a stranger's family line.

"Well, now, that's interesting indeed. Though I do worry about you being in the middle of all of this. It sounds very dangerous, what with you being arrested then stalked by a killer."

Gee, he really knew how to sugarcoat it. "I'm safe as can be, I promise."

"I'd be interested to see this necklace that seems to be the crux of the mystery. We could meet for coffee and go over what you've found so far?"

"I wouldn't want to pull you away from your family."

"I love them dearly, as you well know, but you also know what the ancients said. After three days, fish and houseguests smell bad." He laughed at his own joke. "I could use a little fresh air."

Since it was so close to New Year's Eve, we agreed to meet on January 2nd at the Sip & C'est at eleven, and I returned to my research on the Redfield line.

After a couple of hours, I felt like I was getting absolutely nowhere. I'd made some reasonable, I hoped, assumptions based on documents found, but once I got to the early 1900s, I had no luck finding any further links.

And no where did they appear to cross or connect to the location of Rosemary's line. It stumped me.

Instead, I pulled up my notes on the engraving on the necklace. Perhaps I could make some headway with the mystery message and find a clue there.

Hoping for something to point me in the right direction, I entered the first word "*Dauerhafte*" into the search engine and not only found a definition but a language clue as well. It was German. Which tracked with the genealogy of our family. I wrote "permanent" as my first bit of translation.

Entering each line into a German to English translation tool, I came up with a few words but the sentence made no sense. Some parts didn't seem to translate at all, which was a puzzle all its own.

se, die wir
 ?, we

en, unseren
?, our

zu geben
admit

und Flugel.
and wings.

Permanent, we, our admit and wings.

That was less than enlightening. I'm not sure even the most talented of philosophy students could contrive some meaning from this handful of words. It was like someone took one of those magnetic poetry sets and jumbled them into an engraving order.

I slumped against the back of my chair in disgust. "This is so frustrating!" I moaned to the empty apartment. The pep talk I'd given myself was wearing thin with this second dead end of the day.

Switching gears, yet again, I checked Vincent's social media feeds. Still nothing new. I idly scrolled through his posts until I came to a picture of him at work, in scrubs and a white coat, holding a large dog of indeterminate breed.

His eyes were kind. The doc's. They crinkled in the corners as he smiled at whoever was taking the picture. Or maybe it was the antics of the squirmy dog in his arms. He wore a simple watch but no other jewelry. I saw no rings, at least. He wore wire-rimmed glasses, showed no sign of pierced ears, and had a stethoscope around his neck.

A glint of something at his neckline caught my eye. It was different from the metal pieces of the stethoscope and, when I enlarged the photo a bit, was peeking out from under his scrub top. Could it be a chain?

I scrolled through more photos, looking for a better, higher-resolution image that might show any details of what he wore around his neck. Fifteen minutes later, I found what I was looking for.

He was in profile, fishing from a dock somewhere, sunglasses shading his eyes. The neck of his T-shirt showed the telltale sign of a chain around his neck. This time, I could clearly see the bulky coin-and-link design of the chain through the lightweight fabric.

It matched the look of my own necklace.

In any other situation, I would not be inclined to make this kind of leap. Even now I second-guessed myself, checking again and again to make sure I wasn't seeing only what I wanted to see. While the chain was rather distinctive, I couldn't tell if there was a pendant that looked anything like mine. But adding in the murder and the break-ins, I couldn't help but see the connection between the two pieces of jewelry and, therefore, the two families.

I went back to the family trees I'd been working with. Our line became murky after a generation or two in England. The Redfield line, however, didn't even get that far. Whereas our family had come to the colonies around 1835, the Redfield line didn't show up in the states for another eighty years.

I wished, more than once that day, I knew where the Redfield's were beyond that starting point. People didn't just spring up out of nothing. Identities were rather fluid the farther back you went, though, and someone down the line could have reinvented themselves for whatever reason.

A knock at the door interrupted my scan of Rosemary's ancestors for the umpteenth time.

CHAPTER TWENTY-ONE

Vincent Redfield stood on the other side of the screen door. My eyes flicked to his neckline, but I saw no sign of the heavy chain I'd noticed in the photos. His lips smiled, but his eyes were cold. It was a moment or three before I realized he'd spoken. I had to ask him to repeat himself.

"Are you MC Barker?"

I thought about playing dumb, but there didn't seem to be much point in it. "Yes. And you're Vincent Redfield."

"Good. You know who I am."

"I'm sorry for your loss, Mr. Redfield."

"Oh. Right. Thank you."

"Is that why you're here? Because I found the body—his body—and you had questions? I tried to reach you, but your secretary said you were traveling."

"She mentioned that. May I come in?"

We'd been speaking through the screen door and I balked, briefly, at the thought of letting him in. It was a strange urge, but I chalked it up to paranoia over this whole situation getting the best of me. His showing up like this could answer so many questions. I could at least invite him in.

"Would you like a glass of water? Or I could make some coffee, if you prefer?" I offered as he sat on the blanket-covered sofa.

"No. Thank you." His voice didn't sound like what I thought it would. I'd figured him for a strong tenor, with maybe a western drawl, but he sounded like a pack a day smoker with a knife edge on his vowels. His eyes were harder in person than they'd looked online, and I struggled to recall his brother's eyes over the gas pump only to realize I'd barely made eye contact with the stranger that day. The automatic caution of a woman traveling alone in an unfamiliar city kicking in.

I didn't have that caution now, and neither did he. We sat—him on the sofa, me on one of the kitchen stools—for several moments, studying each other. When I'd had the impulse to contact him, what had I planned to say to him other than condolences? What would I say to him now?

"Did you—"

"How did—" He bowed his head and swept an open palm in my direction. Ladies first.

"Did you have anything specific you wanted to know? I mean, I'm not sure I can offer more than what the police could."

"Yes, I was wondering how you came upon him?"

"I was taking a walk in the woods, along the trails, while visiting some relatives."

"Did you notice anyone else in the woods while you were out there?"

"No, I was pretty sure I was alone. In fact, I was so distracted by the family stuff I must have passed him on the way into the woods. I only noticed the body on my way back to the house."

"I see."

"I thought, at first, I might have been able to do something for him if I'd noticed sooner. But the officer said that he'd been dead a while and moved to the woods just before I found him."

Vincent nodded, but didn't speak. He sat with his head tilted, eyes lidded, watching me through mere slits as I spoke. He was so still during my retelling that I couldn't meet his gaze for long without feeling uneasy.

"Again, I'm very sorry for your loss."

He performed the same slight nod but said nothing. Watching me. I couldn't even be sure if he blinked. This guy was more than a little unnerving. It was a good thing his patients were animals. I'm not sure that sort of bedside manner would go over well with people if he gave them that same penetrating stare.

"Do you know what your brother was doing in Mississippi?" I asked. Maybe he'd be less imposing if he spoke.

"Not really. Duane and I hadn't been speaking a lot lately. He moved around a lot, going from place to place, staying long enough to make things interesting before moving on to someplace new." One side of his mouth quirked up in something between a grin and a sneer.

"I thought twins were supposed to be close."

"In some ways, we were. After all, we look very similar. When we were younger, we could swap places and fool people. But he—well, we ended up wanting different things. And the old man was demanding. Duane didn't like being compared to Vincent all the time and went out to prove who he was on his own.

"With varying degrees of success." Breaking his gaze from my face, he repositioned the heavy silver link bracelet on his wrist. "But I loved my brother as much as I could, because we were the same in a lot of ways."

"Wanda mentioned he was prone to getting into trouble."

Vincent chuckled, his eyes returning to me. "Oh, yes. Trouble was his constant companion. But you should know he only got caught once for every ten escapades."

"You sound almost proud of him for that."

"Why wouldn't I be? It shows he's smarter than people give him credit for. Just because he didn't go to college and work in an office doesn't mean he's ignorant or untalented."

"You speak of him in the present tense."

"What?" Something flickered across his face. "Oh, I guess I did. Still getting used to the idea of him being gone, I guess."

"Have the officers told you any more? Have they figured out who or why he was, uh, killed?"

"No. And I doubt they'll figure it out. They didn't strike me as the brightest bulbs."

I couldn't quite stifle the snort that burbled up. "No, they really didn't. After all, they accused me of it, at first. Which was ludicrous. I'm grateful they realized that, but still."

"Of course it wasn't you. You don't look like you could harm a fly."

The once over his eyes gave me at that point made me wish I was standing on the other side of the small breakfast bar. I was stronger and sturdier than I looked, but I didn't exactly get the impression he was appreciating my body as much as he was sizing me up like a spider to the fly.

But wait, this was my apartment, wouldn't that make me the spider?

I decided to act on my impulse, rounded the bar and took the three steps to the fridge and retrieved a bottle of water. "Are you sure I can't get you anything?" The southern hospitality must be rubbing off on me. I didn't want to offer this man anything. I only wanted him gone.

"What I want isn't in the icebox," a voice far too close to me said.

CHAPTER TWENTY-TWO

I spun around, cornered in the crook of the open refrigerator door.

"Mr. Redfield," I began, struggling for composure. "I'm not sure what you're after, but I think it's about time you left."

"But we were just getting to the good part." Vincent took the bottle of water from my hand and tossed it into the sink before grabbing both my hands and pushing them above my head. "Where's the necklace?"

His face was mere inches from mine. The shiver I felt was not from the cooler at my backside. "I—I don't know what you're talking about."

"Don't play dumb, MC, you're no good at it. I know you have it, and if you give it to me, I'll be gone before you can say boo. If you refuse, well, then I'll just have to stay longer to convince you to hand it over."

"It's not here." I thought of the necklace, snug in its safe deposit box, grateful it was there. At the same time, I feared how he would take the news.

A part of me wished I did have the necklace with me so I could just hand it over and be done with it. That same part of me knew it wouldn't necessarily guarantee my safety.

"You're lying." He glared at me and tightened his grip on my wrists. "It wasn't in your truck and it wasn't here when I searched the place the other night. So you have to be keeping it close by."

He palmed the front of my shirt and I shuddered. Then he checked my jeans pockets and came up empty.

"Maybe you left it with the little blonde lady. Is she keeping it safe for you?"

Well, hell's jingling bells. He'd been watching me long enough to know who Windi was. Jerri was right to insist on her safety, too. And I was forty kinds of a fool for leading this man to our doorsteps. How was I going to get out of this?

Taking a deep breath, I willed my shoulders to relax and looked him straight in the eyes. "Okay, fine. I have it, it's here. I'll get it for you if you'll move out of my way."

"Now that's more like it." He stepped back just enough to allow me to scoot by him. "Glad you decided to see reason."

I was rounding the bar when my phone rang from the counter. I froze as I reached for it out of habit, looking at Vincent to see what he would do.

"Let it go to voicemail."

"They'll worry if I don't answer."

"You think too highly of other people. They'll leave a message and won't give you a second thought."

"It could be important." My stalled hand itched to pick up the phone. Prayed it was someone who could help.

"What's important is you getting me that necklace. Don't worry about the phone."

It had stopped ringing by then, and I resumed heading towards my backpack at the far end of the sofa. If Vincent had thought he was less than five feet from his goal the whole time we sat and talked, would that have made a difference? Would he have what? Knocked me out and stolen it then? Worse?

I kneeled by the pack, fiddling with the zipper, chancing a look over my shoulder to see where he was. He had returned to the sofa but was standing, an expectant look on his face.

"It's an old—" the ringing of my cell phone cut whatever stalling tactic I was going to try. Vincent was in the way of me even thinking about trying to answer it.

"I really should get that."

"You really should get that necklace for me."

I noticed he didn't say anything about calling them back later. After he was gone. Well, I wasn't foolish enough to think he was just going to take his leave and let bygones be or anything. Reaching into the backpack, I rummaged around, as if the necklace had fallen down into the depths of the bag.

I figured I had one chance to do this, and even that chance was slim, as I thumbed on the stun gun Jerri had insisted I charge and carry.

"Hurry up, now, I haven't got all day," Vincent said, closer behind me than he was before.

It happened like we were moving underwater. Still crouched by the end of the sofa, I spun on one foot and braced myself to run with the other as I lifted an empty fabric pouch up to him. In my other hand I held the weapon, which I jammed into the inside of his thigh, as high as I could, in the split second he took his eyes off me and reached for the pouch.

I'd barely lunged out of the way as he crumpled to the ground, cursing and immobilized for just long enough for me to grab my phone and my keys off the bar and slam out of the door.

Time whooshed to catch up with me again. It's a wonder I didn't fall tush over teakettle down the stairs in my hurry, though I'd find a splinter in my palm the next day, once the adrenaline finally wore off.

My plan was to run for the Jeep and head for the sheriff's station, but Jerri was turning onto my street by the time I got to the sidewalk. Instead of heading to my car, I dashed into the street to intercept the SUV.

"You didn't answer my calls. Are you okay?" she shouted as she as she slammed into park and exited the vehicle, hand resting on the pistol as she surveyed the area.

"He's upstairs. I don't think can follow me," I panted, bent at the waist and gulping in air.

"Stay here. Don't move."

Jerri started up the stairs as she announced herself in a low, authoritative voice. When she got to the landing, I saw that I'd somehow dislodged the screen door from the upper hinge and it was hanging askew. Jerri nudged past it, issuing an order to stay where he was with his hands visible.

I held my breath when she moved out of my sight line into the apartment. When I heard no further shouting, scuffle, or shots fired, I wondered if it was safe to follow her. I stayed put. I didn't want to be in the way or get on her bad side (again) for not following directions, so I waited.

It felt like forever before Vincent and Jerri started down the stairs. She steered the hunched figure by his bound wrists as they made their way, awkwardly, to the SUV. Vincent had a pronounced limp. Maybe I should feel bad about that, or at least responsible, but I couldn't find it in me to care at the moment.

That's what he gets for messing with Christmas.

CHAPTER TWENTY-THREE

"Fifteen minutes to midnight!" Molly sang out as the small crowd of local business owners and friends cheered.

The Sip & C'est was not open to the public on New Year's Eve, only to select friends and neighbors who gathered for the annual party to celebrate the ringing in of the new year. We'd already watched the ball drop in Times Square, but being in the central time zone meant we got a whole extra hour of partying before it was officially 2018 in Eden Creek.

While the big party may have been going on across the lake in New Orleans, Molly and Jon had gone all out to outfit us in party hats, glasses, noisemakers, and, of course, beads. And the menu was far from the coffee and pastries of their daily fare. The counter was packed with trays of jambalaya, red beans and rice, crawfish etouffee, boudin, sliced ham, oyster dressing, black-eyed peas and cabbage for health and wealth in the new year, and plenty more besides, leading up to a chocolate fountain and fixings to rival any cruise ship buffet.

"I'm so happy you're here for this, this year!" Windi yelled up to my ear to be heard over the din of people in the café. When I thought back over the last few months, I could only nod in agreement, not trusting my voice to speak.

Compared to other places I've been, the last six months in Eden Creek had been the most amazing. Not just because of the murders and the mysteries—four in all—that I'd had a hand in solving, but the people who had grown on me and, as hard as it was to believe, me onto them. While I didn't know everyone at the party, the ones I did were as important to me as anyone ever had been.

"You know, MC, grandpa worries about you up there by yourself at night," Genevieve, Roscoe's granddaughter, said to me over a glass of punch. "He thinks you should get a dog or something, so you're not so alone."

"A dog would make more messes up there. Besides, I'm not really a dog person."

"Well, a pet of some sort. He doesn't like people being alone." She shrieked as Teddy slung an arm around her neck and kissed her soundly on the cheek. "Isn't that right, Teddy-bear? Doesn't grandpa talk about MC being all alone?"

Teddy grinned at me, blushing only slightly at the nickname. "He does. I think he's more or less adopted you in his head."

"Is he here tonight? I haven't seen him." I scanned the crowd in case he'd been a recent arrival.

"Nah, he's not one for staying up 'til midnight. He watched the feed of the fireworks launched in Australia when they hit midnight over there and called it a day," she laughed.

The young couple ambled off towards the counter for more food, leaving me stunned at how many parents, siblings, and more I'd gained over the last six months. I thought my elderly landlord had been upset with me and regretting me as a tenant a few days ago. Especially when he had to make another trip up the stairs to fix the screen door hinges.

"You need a glass of champagne," Jerri said, handing me the plastic flute.

Speaking of people I thought I'd frustrated beyond tolerance, Jerri had been extra solicitous since Redfield had been arrested and had offered updates on the case's progress without me having to ask. A definite change, all things considered.

—

Once she'd cuffed Vincent, Jerri had called for backup to secure the scene, aka my apartment, and escort me back to the station without making me ride in the same vehicle as the man who'd just tried to steal from me. While I appreciated the consideration, part of me wouldn't have minded giving him a piece of my mind on the way.

We'd called Windi to let her know what was going on, but urged her to stay put with Jasmine. Jerri would take me home whenever she was finished. Hopefully, by then we'd have some answers as to why that necklace was important enough to try to steal it. Perhaps even kill for it?

"We've run into a bit of a problem." Jerri said, handing me a bottle of water.

"He's not going to sue me because I used a stun gun on him, is he? Can he do that?"

"What? No, nothing like that. He called for a lawyer, so we had to wait for one to come in, and now he's claiming that he can't be held accountable for his actions because he's legally dead."

"Is he trying for the insanity defense?"

"If only." Jerri stood and stretched before pacing the short hallway in front of me. The station was otherwise quiet at that time of night, Eden Creek not exactly being rife with crime.

"He claims we arrested Vincent Redfield, which isn't him, because he's actually Duane Redfield. And since Duane Redfield was declared legally dead in Mississippi, he can't be arrested at all because he doesn't, legally, exist."

"And the lawyer is going along with it?"

"He hasn't stopped him yet."

"So what does this mean?"

"That's where the problem comes in." She shrugged her shoulders. "I honestly don't know. Vincent, Duane, whoever he is, assaulted you in your apartment. Which allows us to hold him if you want to press charges—"

"Which I do!"

"I figured as much. We can hold him for that until we can get him in front of a judge. The judge can sort out the who's who legal issue."

They'd found a match to my necklace on Redfield as he was being processed and a quick test concluded it could well be the murder weapon of the other Mr. Redfield. That they were twins was figuring heavily into the discussion of who was really whom in this whole big mess.

"Obviously, I can't let you see the necklace he had since it's, you know, a murder weapon and therefore evidence. But we did take pictures for the file and I made you a copy," she said, handing over the printouts of the front and back of the twin to my own necklace. "Just don't say where you got them."

As if it wouldn't be obvious.

The inscription on this half of the pendant was much easier to read, and I suspected it would help the translation efforts tremendously. The front of the

Redfield necklace was more ornate than mine, and I could see a small indentation on one side and the remains of what appeared to be a hinge on the other. While my half showed neither of these traits, it stood to reason they could have been filed down or worn down over time. It had started out life as a locket, broken apart at some point in the past.

When and why were still up in the air, but there must have been a connection between the two families. One that we would continue to suss out. Though, perhaps, not as urgently as when it seemed we were being stalked.

Despite asking for a lawyer, Duane didn't seem to be all that interested in listening to him. Believing himself to be untouchable because of the identity loophole, he spun out a series of hypotheticals that pretty much told the deputies what he'd done. That he'd switched their identification and posed as his brother was bringing up questions of identity theft and faking his own death into the mix, though the motive was still not entirely clear.

Oh, well, that was for the state and a judge to handle at this point.

—

"This, right here, is why I willingly work every other holiday they ask me to," the deputy said. "Just so I can relax and enjoy New Year's Eve and New Year's Day like a normal human being."

"Does that make New Year's your favorite holiday?"

"Got it in one."

"Why, though?" Working with people in and around academia meant the year started in the fall for me. January first was any other calendar page turn.

"For the same reason you inexplicably like Mondays. It's the promise of a whole new year, a new start." She looked me in the eye and said softly, "New beginnings. New opportunities. A great big heaping helping of second chances, every year."

"Sixty seconds!" Joe bellowed from his perch at the top of a ladder. Why he was on the ladder, no one seemed to care or question. There he sat, surveying the assemblage like a king on his throne.

"The fact that it comes with a great big countdown, bubbles, and silly hats doesn't hurt, either!" Jerri laughed as she put her arm around my shoulders and turned me to face the television on the far wall.

I only registered the countdown clock with the half of my brain not acutely aware of the warmth and weight of Jerri's arm around me, the sound of her soft counting that much closer to my ear, the scent that was a mixture of her detergent and deodorant and shampoo that made her familiar in a way that no one else was.

"Twenty. Nineteen. Eighteen…"

Oh, gosh, it was going to be midnight. People kiss at midnight.

"Seventeen. Sixteen. Fifteen…"

I'd hugged my friends at midnight, sure, the handful of times I'd gone out for the night instead of staying in. Even air kissed a few cheeks. But this crowd was way more riled up and comfortable with one another.

"Fourteen. Thirteen. Twelve…"

I can get away with hugging, right? No one was going to try to kiss me, were they?

"Eleven. Ten. Nine…"

"Y'all pucker up, now!" someone called out as the countdown continued.

"Eight. Seven. Six…"

I wasn't as worried about a near stranger trying to kiss me as I was about the woman standing next to me. Closely. Her voice and glass rising as the numbers fell.

"Five. Four. Three…"

Was I ready for this? Was I overthinking it?

"Two…"

I wouldn't be so nervous if some part of me didn't want it, I realized. I was preoccupied because, holy hand grenades, I actually wanted Jerri to kiss me at midnight.

"One! Happy New Year!"

Around me, everyone cheered. *Auld Lang Syne* played from the speakers mounted around the coffee shop. People toasted, drank, hugged, kissed, and laughed as Joe set off a series of confetti cannons from his perch.

With confetti raining down, time did its slow-crawl again as Jerri's arm fell away from my shoulders, only to be followed by the feel of her hand on the back of my neck. She smiled and slowly leaned in for a gentle kiss.

"Here's to a new start," she whispered in my ear.

Then she was off, hugging and cheering her way through the crowd before I'd even had a chance to process, much less react to, what had just happened. I followed her with my eyes, her height making it easy, as I felt my face reddening.

Windi appeared at my elbow, her arm slipping around my waist. "Did I just see what I think I saw?"

"Yup." Did anyone else see? They were preoccupied with their own celebrating, right? No one was paying attention to us. Right?

"Is there something you need to tell me, Mary Catherine Barker?" She was laughing at me, yes, but not in a mean way.

"I... I honestly don't know."

"Interesting," she said, drawing out the first syllable for a few extra beats. "Very, very interesting."

EPILOGUE

"So. This is worth killing over." The professor and I huddled over steaming cups of coffee and my inherited necklace.

"Apparently so."

"And now you can solve the mystery of the locket's message." He tapped his finger on the photograph showing the engraved twin to my half of the locket.

"It's a line from Goethe. I'll spare you my poor attempt at a German accent and just give you the English. 'There are only two lasting bequests we can hope to give our children. One of these is roots, the other, wings.'"

It'd only been a handful of days since the altercation with Duane posing as Vincent, and parts of the story were still filtering my way.

Despite his attempts to capitalize on a legal loophole as he saw it, Duane's status as a corpse had since been rescinded and he'd been duly arrested as himself after a psychiatric evaluation proved him sane, if not smart. He'd hoped that stepping into his brother's identity would be as simple as it had when the two boys were younger, playing pranks on teachers and parents. His goal had been a fresh start with the advantages he felt had been denied him.

Not that he denied any of his past wrongdoings. Just the unfairness of getting caught so many times.

We would never know what Vincent was planning to do in Mississippi. Why exactly he was looking for our family. Maybe he was looking for a missing branch of his family tree. Or maybe, like Duane, he was looking for the other half of the necklace.

Duane claimed that his family line should be the rightful keeper of the heirlooms, as it was through his paternal line that the original had been created and originally handed down from father to son. It wasn't until one of a pair of twin brothers, what would become Rosemary's line, had immigrated to America that they split the locket into two pieces and began their separate journeys.

That I was in possession of that much information was only because Duane asked his lawyer to talk to me. Not to apologize or anything so honorable. No, he wanted the lawyer to recover the locket half that I had by legal means. Especially since the other half, his half, was in an evidence bag for the foreseeable future.

"The nerve, right?" I shook my head at the whole thing.

"But he gave you more information than you had before, so it wasn't all bad. Now you have a name to research to find where the family split."

"Does it even matter at this point?"

"Eh. Maybe it doesn't feel like it now, but you, or your mother, or your grandmother, might want to know. Might want more information about where they came from." He scrutinized me for a moment. "You know... This would make an interesting chapter—"

"Lemme stop you right there, Professor. This is not open to public consumption. I'm happy being on the sidelines in your research project, not a bug under the historical microscope."

"Hmm. We'll see."

I walked back to my apartment later that afternoon, looking forward to the start of the new semester and the work to come. And continuing to deny the professor's request to include my family's story as an example in his book. Part of my job as his research assistant was to help him stay on one track, after all.

I had to excuse myself to get by the guy sitting on the steps leading to my apartment. I didn't give him more than a passing thought, figuring he was waiting on someone in Up a Creek, until I heard footsteps following me up the stairs.

"Can I help you?" I wondered how fast I could get to the stun gun in the pocket of my backpack as I turned to face the man. He looked familiar, but not in a way I could immediately place. Still, after all that had happened, I was more than a little wary of strangers coming to my door.

"I'm looking for a Mary Catherine Barker. Am I in the right place?"

"Depends on who you are." It felt corny to say, like something from a bad television show, but a girl couldn't be too cautious. I was learning. The hard way, maybe, but learning just the same.

"Well, I'm her brother."

LAGNIAPPE

A little something extra…

The Mother (aka The Empress)

Traditionally known as The Empress, this card of the Major Arcana exemplifies the warmth, nurturing, and protectiveness of the mothers and mother-goddesses throughout multiple pantheons. So we feel confident in renaming this card The Mother for our deck.

She is not only the mother of children, but of ideas, projects, and prosperity. She represents a sense of stability and security we need to build a foundation for whatever endeavors we pursue. And though she is an emotion-centered card, her realm is that of the five senses, as opposed to the High Priestess (Intuition) that comes before her.

Like many mothers, she can be a card of indulgence, but at the same time this cards asks us to be patient as we create new things. After all, babies take time to gestate, and so do ideas and new works. The Mother is a wonderful card to connect with on a new business venture or creative project.

Symbols to look for on representations of The Empress or Mother include the stars above her head (the abundance of stars in the sky, the constellations, the zodiac), some form of the feminine symbol ♀ (sometimes as the globe and cross or pomegranate, here we show it on the border of the blanket across her lap), and an eagle or wings (representing strength, freedom, and power).

Reversed, the Mother may be seen as barren, unproductive, or overly dependent on others and not able to stand on her own. It could indicate a creative block or a need for self-care to soothe the soul.

Other interpretations of this card, when reversed, would include overindulgence or a domineering personality. It could indicate a lack of nurturing energy to full-on rejection. Or it could indicate difficulty in expressing emotions and desires.

Not all reversed cards are negative, however. Depending on the placement in a reading, the reversed Mother could mean taking a more logical approach to the issue at hand instead of an emotional.

As we use the cards as tools of introspection, your own thoughts and experiences with the role of mothers, guides, or nurturing can absolutely play a part in the interpretation whenever this card comes up (or reversed) in a reading.

The Problem Pyramid

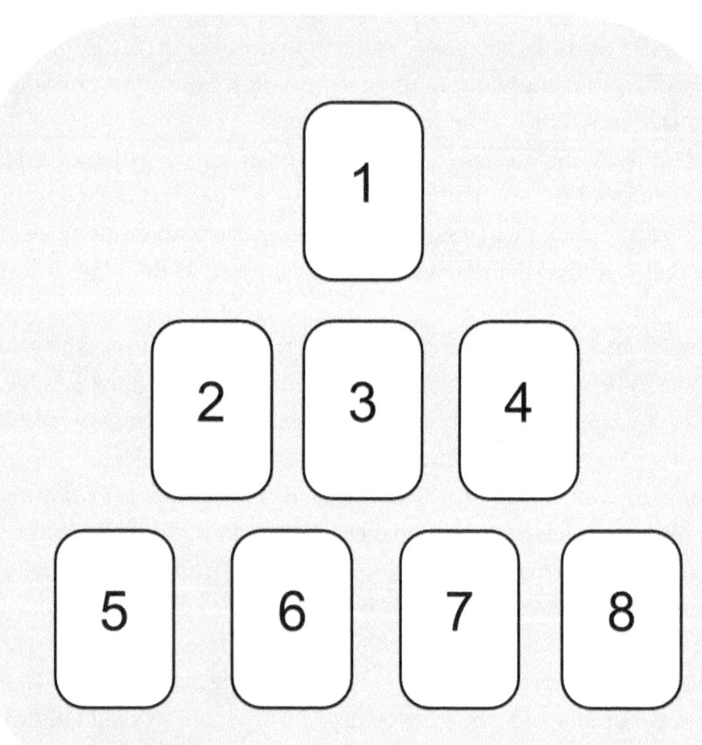

1: The Problem
2: The Past
3: The Present
4: The Future
5: The Root of the Problem
6: The Motivation Behind the Problem
7: The Obstacles in the way of Solving the Problem
8: The Potential Outcome

I created the Problem Pyramid spread for this book, but it has it's roots in many common spreads. You may recognize some position descriptions from The Celtic Cross, for instance, as well as the common Past-Present-Future three-card spread.

That's the wonderful thing about tarot readings: you can build the spread to suit the issue at hand.

This spread tackles an issue from the top down, digging deeper into the whys and hows behind a thing. That's how I like to approach problems, and, well, MC seemed to inherit that from me. Call it an author's prerogative.

As you deal the cards into each position, look at how they interact with each other, as well as with their position on the board. As we see in MC's earlier reading where most of the cards she dealt for the family were reversed, signaling a trend of secrets, blockages, or stifling of emotions.

If you need more answers, consider adding another card to the positions that need some additional insight. Just because there are eight positions listed, doesn't mean you're restricted to only eight cards. The thing to watch out for is dealing cards until you get the one you want. That's the opposite of gaining insight from the cards or a spread such as this.

Rum Balls

One of my favorite childhood memories from Louisiana was when the women in the family gathering in the kitchen to make cookies, candies, etc., for the holidays. Date loaf, divinity, pralines, and, best of all, rum balls. Sometimes people use bourbon or whiskey instead of rum, so select your spirit based on your preference.

—

- 2 ½ cups crushed vanilla wafers
- 2 Tbsp cocoa powder
- 1 cup powdered sugar, plus more for rolling
- 1 cup chopped pecans (or sub with more crushed wafers)
- 3 Tbsp honey
- ¼ cup rum

In a large bowl, combine the crushed cookies, cocoa, 1 cup of the powdered sugar, and the nuts (if you're using them). Stir in honey and rum and mix until a sticky dough forms, adding more wet ingredients if necessary. Roll into 1-inch balls and coat each in the additional powdered sugar. Store in an airtight container.

Makes approximately 3 dozen.

—

The rest of that childhood memory, by the way, included being allowed to have one or two rum balls before they were all put away into a stainless-steel canister in the walk-in pantry. Sometime later, the grown-ups found me in the pantry, in the dark, with the container of rum balls. I probably slept well that night.

Author's Note

When preparing for this book, I had to do some back of the envelope generational math to figure out when the different halves of MC's ancestors were likely to have come to America. Not to mention when Veronica would have graduated high school, and when she would have had Maxine and Roger to make their ages make sense.

This went far beyond the vague notions I had already built out about when MC was born (1986) and when she and Windi graduated college (2007) to make the first few books work. Now there's a whole spreadsheet with names and dates and all sorts of information in it. I imagine it will grow as the story continues.

There were many ways the family side of the conflict could occur, and wrangling those ideas into something that would make sense in a mystery that was not meant to be a historical tale made for several starts and restarts. I appreciate your patience while I sorted out all the options that came with adding a whole passel of family into the mix.

The inscription on the necklaces was one I found while looking for German quotes from the 1830s or before. In my mind, it seemed fitting to have the separating family pass on something that spoke of giving children roots and wings. Any translation errors are wholly mine by way of Google translate.

Goethe was the earliest source for it I could find, but it's been quoted by many people since then. I even had a moment of panic when I thought I'd misread my research notes and pulled a quote from an American preacher who didn't say it until Rosemary's Great-great-great-great-grandmother would have moved to this country.

Cajun Night Before Christmas is an actual book I remember from my childhood in Louisiana. If you want a true vernacular delight, look it up next holiday season.

Finally, for anyone curious about another location-specific reference that was mentioned in this story, a rougarou is the Cajun version of a werewolf. It hunts the swamps and bayous for misbehaving children, similar to a lot of cautionary tales.

About the Author

JL Vanderbeek is a writer, illustrator, and mixed media artist living in southwest Georgia. She created Eden Creek from early childhood memories of growing up in southeast Louisiana, mixed with her current life in a charming rural Georgia town. Her fascination with tarot cards goes back several decades.

We're so glad to have you back with us in Eden Creek.

If you haven't guessed by now, each book of the Eden Creek Cozy Mystery series is loosely themed around or tied to a card in the Major Arcana. Since there are twenty-two cards in that portion of a tarot deck, we have a lot more stories to tell.

To be the first to hear when MC, Windi, and the rest have their next story to share, sign up for our newsletter:

www.thecraftybranch.com/newsletter

Subscribers will also have access to a MC and Windi prequel short story as well as other downloadable goodies each month.

If you enjoyed this book, please consider leaving a review on our Amazon page. Even a sentence or two helps others find out about Eden Creek and this party is all about the more, the merrier!

Thank you!

Also from the Author

EDEN CREEK COZY MYSTERY SERIES

Fool's Paradise
Magic Beans
Fluid Intuition
Mother Mayhem

NONFICTION
(as Jennifer Vanderbeek)

What to Feed Your Raiding Party, the comic book cookbook for gamers
(trivia: Jennifer has a culinary degree and is a big geek!)

ADULT COLORING BOOKS
(as Jennifer Vanderbeek)

Sammy the Snaggletooth Sidewinder Wants to be a Star
Posh Pumpkins
Winter Whimsies
Just Desserts